THE MOUNTAINS
HAVE A SECRET

Arthur Upfield was born in England in 1888. When he was twenty-three he emigrated to Australia, and during the First World War he served with the Australian Army. After the war he roamed Australia, working as a boundary-rider, offside driver, cattle-drover, rabbit-trapper, and cattle station manager. He got to know the Aborigines and their customs, and this material later appeared in his *Bony* novels. The half-aboriginal sleuth, Detective Napoleon Bonaparte, is based on a character Upfield knew well. Many *Bony* novels have appeared since the first in 1951, and they have also formed the basis for a television series.

Arthur Upfield died in 1965.

ARTHUR UPFIELD

THE MOUNTAINS
HAVE A SECRET

Pan Books Sydney and London
in association with William Heinemann

First published 1952 by William Heinemann Limited
This edition published 1983 by Pan Books (Australia) Pty Limited
68 Moncur Street, Woollahra, New South Wales
in association with William Heinemann Limited

All rights reserved
ISBN 0 330 27040 0

Printed and bound in Australia by the Dominion Press Hedges and Bell, Melbourne

CHAPTER I

BONY TAKES A GUN

WHEN beyond Glenthompson, Detective-Inspector Napoleon Bonaparte first saw the Grampians. They rose from the vast plain of golden grass; in the beginning, isolated rocks along the north-west horizon, rising to cut sharply into the cobalt sky. The rocks united and upon that quarter of the plain it could be seen that a cosmic hurricane had lashed the earth and created a sea, a sea of blue-black waves poised to crash forward in graphitical suds.

Distance presented mystery, released the imagination, stirred the memory. Beneath those curling wave crests surely dwelt the Beings of Australia's Alcheringa Era, or where perhaps await the Valkyries of the Norsemen to carry the remains of heroes into the Halls of their Valhalla.

Bonaparte had observed mountains rise above the limits of Inland Plains; rounded mountains and rugged mountains, but never mountains like these. The straight and level road seemed to be afraid of these Grampians, appeared to edge him away from them.

It was early in March and the day was hot and still. The highway was lost before and behind in the heat mirage which had no power over the advancing mountains. After the old tourer came a voice which had spoken these words in Melbourne early the previous day:

"Got a gun in your kit? No! I'll get you one. One of my own. Easy to handle—easy to conceal. Take my car. I'll have New South Wales number-plates put on it. You'd better be a Riverina pastoralist on holiday. Keep what happened to Price in your mind all the time you're among those mountains."

The blue-black waves came rolling over the golden plain towards the eager Bonaparte. He was inclined to stop and watch them. The voice of Superintendent Bolt, Chief of the C.I.B., again came winging along the road.

"Persons are always disappearing. Most of 'em because they

want to, and some because they are bumped off and successfully planted. Persons disappear singly; it's rare that two or more disappear together. Two young women went by train to Dunkeld and from there set off on a hike through the Grampians. They reached a pub called Baden Park Hotel, stayed there a couple of days. After they left that pub they were never seen again.

"That was October twenty-second last. They weren't fools in the bush. They carried camping gear, and they had tucker for emergencies. The country is laced with running streams. Not a solitary sign of them was found after they left Baden Park Hotel.

"Weeks after the search was stopped, young Price went into the Grampians. He was one of our promising young men. Born in the Gippsland mountains. Stayed at the Baden Park Hotel for ten or eleven days. He was found dead in his car twenty-five miles away. Shot dead. No connection with the young women, so my officers think. I don't know. I'm not sure about that. If you're interested, memorise the summary. Take a gun—take a gun—take this one. It comes easy into your fist."

Dunkeld came swimming through the heat-waves to welcome Bony, a township old and crinkly, but natty as were the men and the women who first came this way with their bullock drays. Just beyond the shallow valley to the north stood the first of the mountains, facing sheerly to the east, its long western slope massed with trees.

Bony found the hotel, before which he parked his borrowed car on the place where, for a hundred years, coaches had stood whilst the passengers took refreshment and the horses were changed. The small bar being empty of customers, he drank a glass of beer with the landlord and discussed the district so beloved by artists. Following lunch, he announced that he would look round the township, and so came to the police station and entered.

"Glad to meet you, sir," Senior Constable Groves told him. "Heard about your coming from Headquarters. Anything I can do?"

His visitor having seated himself beside the littered desk, Groves surveyed him, noting with shrewd grey eyes the gabardine slacks, the open-necked shirt, the dark brown arms, and

6

the fingers which at once were employed making a cigarette. Without raising his gaze from the task, Bony said:

"Yes. Please report that I arrived here today and left again this afternoon. I am going on to Baden Park Hotel. D'you know why I am here?"

"No, sir, although I could make an easy guess. I've been instructed to render all assistance and to supply you with everything you may call for."

A match was held to the cigarette and, through the resultant smoke, Groves saw a pair of brilliant blue eyes examining him with expressionless intensity. The smoke drifted ceilingwards and warmth entered the blue eyes. The policeman wondered. The slight, lounging figure was not in focus with the picture of a detective-inspector painted for him by his superiors.

"I am interested in the fate of the two young ladies who disappeared in the Grampians last October," Bony slowly said. "After the thorough search for them, I don't expect to discover much of value. Still, I have succeeded in similar cases. Might I expect your collaboration?"

"Certainly, sir," Senior Constable Groves replied warmly. "I'll be only too glad to do whatever I can."

"Thank you. Please begin by giving me your private opinion of the motive for the murder of Detective Price."

"I believe that Price was killed because he chanced to meet and recognise a dangerous criminal who was touring or who was a member of a large road gang camped near the place where he was shot."

"You don't think it might have any connection with the disappearance of the two girls?"

Groves shook his head and glanced towards the large-scale map affixed to the wall. Bony abruptly left his chair and crossed to the map, Groves standing beside him.

"There's the Grampians," he said. "Fifty-odd miles from north to south and twenty-five-odd miles from east to west. Here's Dunkeld down here at the southern edge. There's Hall's Gap away up on the northern edge. Three miles from Hall's Gap was where they found Detective Price. The girls were lost twenty-five miles south of the place where Price was murdered, and approximately in the middle of the mountains. Have you ever been in them?"

"No. Point out the road taken by the two girls."

7

"Well, from Dunkeld down here, they took the road northward past Mount Abrupt, which you can see through the window. They left about nine in the morning, and at eight that night a truck-driver saw them camped beside the road where there's a little creek. Twenty miles from Dunkeld. The next——"

"The truck-driver? Where had he come from?"

"From Baden Park Station—here."

"Oh! Proceed."

"The next morning the girls followed the road to Hall's Gap for a further ten miles where there's a bridge and a turn-off track to the Baden Park Hotel. There! See the creek?"

"Yes. That turn-off track appears to be secondary to the road to Hall's Gap."

"Yes, it is," Groves agreed. "When they left the hotel here, the girls said they were going through to Hall's Gap, but on reaching the turn-off at the bridge they must have changed their minds. There's a signpost there saying that Baden Park Hotel is four miles away. They had a road map, and therefore they probably saw that they could take that turn-off track, stay at the hotel, go on to the guest-house at Lake George, and from there follow a track which would bring them again to the Hall's Gap Road. I suppose you know all this, sir?"

"Never mind. You tell the story."

"Well. The girls reached the Baden Park Hotel the day after they left Dunkeld. They stayed at the hotel for two days. The licensee telephoned to the guest-house at Lake George and arranged accommodation for them for one night. They left his hotel about ten and had to walk only three and a half miles to the guest-house.

"The next afternoon the guest-house rang the hotel to say that the girls hadn't arrived, but no anxiety was felt at the hotel because the girls had camp equipment and tucker. Two further days passed before the hotel licensee set out to look for them. He could not find them, and the following day he organised a search. They——"

"Describe the search, please," Bony cut in.

"Yes—all right. Er—having ridden along the road to Lake George and not finding any place where the girls had camped, the licensee reported the matter to me that evening. We arranged that he would contact Baden Park Station and ask

8

for riders to get busy early the next morning, and I would take two men with me by car. I and my party reached the hotel at daybreak the next morning. We scoured the bush alongside the road, and the riders from the Station worked farther out. It's hellish country. We kept at it for two weeks, but we found just nothing."

"And then, two months afterwards, Detective Price tried his hand," Bony supplemented.

"Price came in here one afternoon and said he was making for Baden Park Hotel to look round on the off-chance of finding something of the girls. He stayed there ten days. The guest-house people saw him pass their place on his way to Hall's Gap. That was late in the afternoon prior to the morning he was found shot in his car."

"Did the hotel licensee know he was a detective?"

"Yes. He let Price ride his horses. He said that, as far as he knew, Price found no signs of the missing girls. He also said that Price had given up the idea of finding anything of them when he left the hotel."

"How long have you been stationed here?" Bony asked, and was told for ten years. "What is your personal opinion of the licensee?"

Groves frowned at the map before replying.

"The original licensee is Joseph Simpson, an old man and a chronic invalid. He settled there forty or more years ago. There's never been anything against him, or against the son, James, who has been running the place for the last fifteen years. The son is a bit flash, if you know what I mean. Nothing against him, though. He gambles and runs an expensive car. There is a sister about thirty, and a mother who does the cooking. Usually a yard-man is employed."

"Does the position of the hotel warrant the licence?"

"Yes and no," replied Groves. "There's fishing to be had at Lake George, and parties stay at the hotel in preference to the guest-house. I have the idea that the drinking is pretty wild at times, but the place is too isolated for proper supervision. However, the Simpson family are quite respectable citizens and thought well of by Mr. Benson of Baden Park Station."

"The Simpsons' nearest neighbours are the Lake George guest-house?"

"It's a toss-up whether they or the Bensons are the nearer."

9

"The Bensons! What are they in? Sheep or cattle?"

"Sheep," Groves replied, a note of astonishment in his voice. "They breed the famous Grampian strain. Baden Park comprises about thirty thousand acres. There's lashings of money. I was out there several years ago. The Bensons used to own the hotel property."

"H'm!" Bony crossed to the window and gazed beyond at Mount Abrupt, warm and colourful in the sunlight, the serrated mountains beyond it darkly blue and mysterious. "The Bensons? What of them?"

"They don't entertain much or interest themselves in the district's doings," Groves said. "The present Benson isn't married. His sister lives with him. The father was quite a famous astronomer. He built his own observatory near the house, and it must have cost a fortune. The son didn't follow it up, though. I heard that he'd sold the telescope. All he thinks about is breeding, and all he worries over is keeping his sheep from sheep stealers. Can't blame him for that when he breeds rams which fetch a thousand guineas."

"How many men does he employ, d'you know?"

"Not many, I think. Anything from six to a dozen."

"Is sheep stealing prevalent?"

"Not at this time. Petrol rationing restricts that game. But before the war sheep stealing was very bad. You know, men operating fast trucks, pull up, over the fence, grab and grab, and off back to the city. Benson built a strong fence round his place and took other measures to defeat the thieves."

Bony offered his hand.

"I'll be going along to Baden Park Hotel," he said. "Under no circumstances communicate with me. I'm a New South Wales pastoralist enjoying a long-delayed holiday. By the way, how did the guest-house people recognise Price's car that day he passed?"

"Price had run over there twice during his stay at the hotel."

CHAPTER II

AT THE BADEN PARK HOTEL

HAVING rounded Mount Abrupt, Bony drove northwards along a narrowing valley skirted by the frozen land waves. Either side of the road, the gums reached high above the dense scrub and exuded their scent into the warm, still air, but above them the menacing granite face of the ranges betrayed no secrets.

Round a bend appeared the white-painted arms of a long wooden bridge and, on the near end, a signpost standing sentinel at the junction of a track with the road. Straight on was Hall's Gap—twenty miles. Dunkeld lay behind thirty miles. A third arm pointed to the turn-off track and stated that that way was to Baden Park Hotel—four miles—and Lake George—seven and a half miles.

Humming an unrecognisable tune, Bony took the turn-off track, narrow, rough, walled with scrub. There was a faint smile in his eyes and in his heart the thrill of expectancy which drives on the born adventurer.

There are no bushlands in the vast Interior comparable with this, but then, in the Interior, there are no easy landmarks like these ranges. The track dipped gently downwards, and Bony had merely to touch the accelerator. Now and then he passed a crack in the bush walls, cracks which could be enticing to the inexperienced hiker.

The change was almost instantaneous. In the one instant the walls of scrub crowded upon the car; in the next they had vanished and the car was rolling across a large clearing on the left of which stood the hotel, its weather-boarded walls painted cream and its iron roof a cap of terra-cotta. Across the clearing ran a little creek spanned by another but much smaller white-painted bridge.

Bony stopped the car before the veranda steps. To the left of them wistaria covered the lower portion of the veranda and climbed the roof supports. To the right, windows bore the golden letters of the word "Bar". It was a comfortable building, a welcoming building to the traveller. He switched off the engine and heard a voice say:

"Get to hell outa here."

Another voice croaked:

"That's enough of that."

To which the first countered with:

"Nuts! What about a drink?"

From the fly-wired door above the steps emerged a man dressed in a sports shirt and grey slacks. He came down to meet the traveller alighting from the old single-seater. Under forty, his still handsome face bore unmistakable signs of high-pressure living. Shrewd, cold grey eyes examined the visitor even as the sensuous mouth widened into a not unattractive smile.

"Good day!" he said, his accent unexpectedly good. There was a question-mark behind the greeting, as though a stranger coming this way was rare.

"Good day-ee!" Bony replied with an assumed drawl. "You're the landlord, I take it. Can you put me up for a day or two? Pretty place. Looks peaceful."

"Peaceful enough—most times," was the qualified agreement, accompanied by a meaning smile. "Oh yes, we can give you a room. My name is Simpson. Call me Jim."

"Good! I hate formality. My name's Parkes. Call me John. Bar open?"

"It's always open to visitors. Come on in. We can garage your car and bring in your luggage any old time."

Bony followed Simpson to the veranda, and the great yellow-crested cockatoo in its cage suspended from the veranda roof politely asked:

"What abouta drink?"

Farther along the veranda a human wreck in a wheeled invalid chair called out:

"Good day to you!"

"Good day to you, sir," replied Bony.

The invalid propelled his chair forward and Bony paused on the threshold of the door to gaze down into the rheumy eyes of a man past seventy, faded blue eyes gleaming with the light of hope. The white hair and beard badly needed trimming.

"My father," said Simpson within the doorway. "Suffers a

lot from arthritis. Gentleman's name is Parkes, Father. Going to stay a few days."

"What abouta drink?" shrieked the cockatoo.

The old man raised his head, failed to obtain the required angle, spun his chair until he did, and then shook a bony fist at the bird. Fury twisted his slavering mouth and his voice was like a wire in wind.

"If I could get outa this chair I'd wring yer ruddy neck."

To which the bird made a noise remarkably similar to that described as a "raspberry".

The son chuckled and Bony stepped into a small hall, to be surprised by several large oil-paintings on the walls and a large-scale pictorial map of the locality, which at once promised to be interesting. Part way along the passage beyond, Simpson showed the new guest into a small lounge off which could be seen the bar. Here it was dim and cool, and the floor and furniture gleamed like ebony from constant polishing. Bony called for beer and suggested that Simpson join him. Simpson said:

"Come from Melbourne?"

"I don't live there," replied Bony. "Don't like it and wouldn't live in a city for all the wool in Australia. I own a small place out of Balranald. In sheep, but not big. Haven't had a spell for years and I'm enjoying one now, just dithering about here and there."

"The Gramps are different to your class of country, I suppose?"

"They're certainly that. I lease a hundred thousand acres, and I can see across the lot of it with a pair of binoculars, it's that flat. Fill them up, will you? You get many people this way?"

"Not so many," replied Simpson from the pump. "Mostly regulars. Come once or twice every year, chiefly for the fishing at Lake George, and to get off the apron-strings for a necessary change." He set the glasses upon the narrow counter between bar and lounge and lit a cigarette. "The tourists don't come this side of the Gramps. Country's not opened up like it is over at Hall's Gap. Our visitors are solid and good spenders, and in between parties we have an easy time of it."

"The place is probably all the more attractive on that

13

count," averred Bony. "What's the road like across to Hall's Gap?"

"It was only opened last year," replied Simpson, exhaling smoke and calmly regarding his guest. "It's still rough and dangerous for cars with faulty brakes. A hundred thousand acres you have! Lot of country. How many sheep d'you run?"

"Oh, round about ten thousand. It's not like the country I've crossed since leaving Melbourne, you know. Still, it provides a living."

Simpson chuckled and took the glasses back to the pump.

"Better than hotel-keeping," he said. "By the way, you might find the old man a bit of an 'ear basher', but don't let him worry you. He'll put it on you for a drink, but you'd oblige by knocking him back. Booze has been his ruin, and now he's not quite right. Says silly things and imagines the world's against him, and all that."

The refilled glasses were set down on the counter. Beyond this quiet room were occasional sounds: the screech of the cockatoo, the cawing of a passing crow, the clang of a tin bucket, the crowing of a rooster. To Bony the atmosphere was familiar, but there was a shade of difference between this hotel and those others beside the Outback tracks. For one thing, there was no dust in this place, and for another the pictures in the hall were too good to be housed by such a building and too large to adorn so small a hall.

There was an oddity about Simpson too. In view of the fact that there had been no guests prior to his own arrival, the licensee seemed to be too neat and too expensively dressed. Groves had said of Simpson that he was a "bit flash", and doubtless the phrase was meant to apply to the man's habitual appearance.

Despite the evidence of fast living, Simpson was still athletic in movement, and the dynamic depths of his character could be felt by the sensitive Bony. He said:

"Like to see your room?"

The room was entirely to Bony's liking, the window opening on to the veranda whereon the invalid reigned in his wheelchair. They went out to the car and garaged it, and Simpson assisted the new guest with his luggage, proving himself a warm host, and afterwards showing the way to the bathrooms and quoting the meal schedule.

"We usually have dinner about half-past six when times are quiet," he said. "If you don't want another drink just now, I'll do a few jobs waiting my attention. Might take a ride on a horse I've bought. Haven't tried him out yet."

Bony assured him that he would be quite all right, and, having unpacked things for immediate use, he made his way out of the building by a side door and crossed to the bridge spanning the creek. The sun was westering, its rays painting with amber and grey the iron face of the range towering high beyond the hotel it threatened to engulf. There was a track going away past the hotel towards the range which could not be beyond a mile away.

About the hotel and the clearing which it lorded was an outer silence emphasised the more by the small sounds living within it. The singing of the little water went on and on, accompanying the voices of hidden birds, the barking of a dog, the cry of the cockatoo. Three minutes later, seeming to emerge from the outer silence, came the humming of a car engine, low and almost musical.

At first Bony could not pick up its direction. The sound died away, lived again for a moment, and again sank into oblivion. A long thirty seconds passed before he heard it once more, and then could decide that the machine was somewhere at the foot of the range. Presently he saw it swiftly appear from the back-drop of bush and come gliding towards the hotel along the track which skirted the creek. It stopped at the side of the building, and Simpson appeared at that door by which Bony had left.

Although not "car-minded", Bony saw that the machine was a particularly sumptuous Rolls-Royce. A uniformed chauffeur was at the wheel, the passengers being a man and a woman. Simpson walked to the side of the car and spoke to those within through the open window. What he said Bony could not hear, and it was the woman who betrayed the fact that he was speaking of the new guest—a mere involuntary movement of her face.

Then Simpson was standing back, standing upright, stiffly. The car began to move. It curved past the corner of the building to cross the clearing, and Bony received the impression of

a stern masculine face and that of a woman distinctly handsome. The woman did not look at him, but the man did with
one swift sidewise glance. The bush swallowed them and the
car on its way to Dunkeld.

In all probability they were the Bensons of Baden Park, but
their identity was of less import to Bony than the obvious fact
that his map was inaccurate. On his map, the turn-off to
Baden Park Station was half a mile beyond the bridge, on the
road to Lake George, and not at the hotel.

He lingered on the bridge for five minutes or more before
sauntering to the front veranda steps where he was greeted by
the cockatoo with "Nuts!" There were chairs backed against
the wall, and he sat in one near old Simpson, who visibly
brightened at the prospect of talking with someone.

"A beautiful place and a beautiful day," Bony commented.

" 'Tis so," agreed the ancient indifferently. The tired eyes
took in the new guest from his black hair to his shoes, and into
them crept that gleam of hope. "You got any brass?"

The Yorkshireman's name for money was startling, for there
was no trace of the Yorkshire accent in the quavering voice.

"Not very much," he was told, Bony recalling the request
made by the son.

"Pity. No one seems to have any money. You got any
guts?"

"Not much of that, either. Supposing I had—if you mean
courage?"

The old man glanced furtively at the open window next to
Bony's bedroom. Then he moved his chair closer and whispered:

"I know where there's lashings of booze. Jim and Ferris are
going off to Dunkeld tonight, and the old woman goes to bed
about ten. What say we raid the spirit store? It's only just
along the passage and I've got a key. Had it for years. They
never found it on me. They don't know I've got it. Inside the
store there's stacks of whisky and brandy and wine—stacks
and stacks. Let's have a night tonight, eh? I ain't had a real
drink in years and I'm as dry as a wax match. We could lock
ourselves in there and drink and drink. Shall us?"

The voice was coaxing, wheedling. The eyes were now wide
and imploring. The prisoner in the chair was a prisoner in a
dying body. What an escape the prisoner envisaged, what an

escape for an hour or so! There was pity in Bonaparte's heart but no relenting, although he said:

"I must think it over."

"Think it over!" scoffed the old man. "Think over a proposition like that! Free grog and as much as you can down in a coupler hours! And you want to think it over! The modern generation's soft, that's what it is. No guts—no—no—— What d'you say your name is?"

"Call me John. What's the matter with you?"

"With me!" was the indignant echo. "Nothin's the matter with me, young feller, exceptin' me arthritis and a touch of gout now and then and a hell of a dry throttle. I've got good health and plenty of guts, and I ain't afeared of raidin' a spirit store like you are. There's the ruddy spirit store and I got a key to it. All I wants you to do is to go there with me after the old woman's in bed and open the door for me 'cos I can't get up at the lock. I tell you there ain't nuthin' wrong with me."

"Nuts!" murmured the cockatoo with astonishing appropriateness. It mumbled something and then yelled: "What abouta drink?"

CHAPTER III

THE PRISONERS

"REACH me down that fowl," pleaded old Simpson. "Lemme get the feel of his neck in me hands. They only hang him up there to mock at me and put on me the evil eye. They don't want me to get well and be the master in me own house."

Tears of self-pity rolled down his withered cheeks and into the unkempt white whiskers, and Bony said:

"Have you lived here very long?"

A palsied forearm was drawn across the watering eyes; the old man's lips trembled. Bony looked away for a moment or two and then was presented with a picture of youth and virility and courage.

"Afore you was born," came the words of the picture, "me and the old woman came here back in the year one. There was no roads to anywhere then once we left Dunkeld, only a bit of track coming through these mountains to get into Baden Park. Every mile of that track was harder than twenty miles over plain country."

Memory was wiping away the ravages of the years, over-laying the features with a make-up to re-create a man of yesteryear. The voice lost its quavering, was steady, and the eagerness of the pioneer flared into the light blue eyes.

"I was young in them days, and the old woman was younger than me. I druv six bullocks in a dray and she druv four horses to a buckboard. She was carryin' Alf, too. Took us all of a fortnight to make the thirty miles. I had to build two bridges in them weeks, but Kurt Benson promised me land and a fair go if we could make it.

"We made it all right, and just in time. Settled right here beside the crick. The clearing here now was a clearing then, and when we had let the bullocks and the horses go that first evening, the old woman got her pains. It was raining like hell and cold. They want hospitals now and doctors. Soft, that's what they are now.

"Any'ow, we cleared the land back from the crick and grew grapes and fruit. Benson, the present man's father, was a good man and true. He helped us all he could, and later on he got us the licence and set us up, advertising in the papers for us, helping with the track and all.

"The first child got drowned in the crick when he was three, and Jim came along then and afterwards Ferris. We did well, me and the old woman. This all belongs to me, you unnerstand, and I ain't dead yet. Jim's been at me for years to give it to him, but there ain't a chance. I signed a will and they don't know where it is. They'd like to know, but they never will, not until after I'm gone. If they knew where that will is they'd burn it, and one night they'd leave the door of the spirit store open."

"What for?" Bony asked without keen interest, for the story he had heard was not an uncommon one. The old man's voice sank to a sibilant whisper.

"So's I'd get inside and drink and drink and drink and never come out any more. Then I'd be another body in that spirit store, all stiff and cold. You wouldn't let me stay in there and drink and drink until I was dead, would you? You listen and talk to me, you do. The others won't. Jim won't let 'em. Jim tells 'em that I'm balmy, he tells 'em I imagines things. He calls 'em away from me and leaves me to be tormented by that ruddy fowl. And his mother's back of him."

The cockatoo whirred its wings and screeched, and it was as though the cacophony wiped off the make-up, burned out the re-created man.

"Get to hell outa here!" yelled the bird.

The wistaria hid the veranda steps from Bony and the invalid, and they did not observe the approach of two men who came up the steps. They were dressed in riding-breeches, brown boots and leggings, and both were wearing wide-brimmed felts. Spurs jangled. One of the men laughed. They were young and lean and hard and stained darkly by the sun and the wind.

"What about a drink?" each asked of the cockatoo, the first with a foreign accent, the second with the clipped tones of a city-bred man. The bird replied with a rasberry and hung upside-down. When the men had entered the building the old man whispered:

19

"They're Benson's men."

There was no apparent reason why the information should be so announced. The voice was tainted by fear, but there was no fear in the old eyes now regarding Bony with clear steadiness. He fancied that he saw mockery in them.

"D'you get many callers?" he asked, and the previous expression of self-pity flashed into the withered face.

"Not this time of year. Christmas and Easter we're full up to the doors. They don't let me sit here them times—not now. Didn't mind it much when Ted O'Brien was workin' here and me and Ted uster talk about the old days. But Jim got rid of Ted. Said he drank too much. Caught him dead drunk in the spirit store first thing one mornin'." The tears again rolled downwards into the whiskers. "Ain't got no one to talk to since Ted O'Brien was sacked. You'll talk to me, won't you? You won't believe I'm balmy and steer clear of me, eh? Let's be cobbers, and one night we can raid the spirit store. Let's raid it tonight. Jim and Ferris are going to Dunkeld tonight. I heard Ferris tell the old woman about it."

The conversation fell away into a monologue of complaints, and presently the two riders came out, followed by Jim Simpson. For a little while they stood above the veranda steps, talking in low voices, and when the man had gone Simpson came along to Bony and the old man. His smile did not include his father.

"We'll be serving dinner at six tonight, because my sister and I are going to town," he said. "It's half-past five. Will you be wanting a drink before dinner? I'm asking because I'd like to get dressed."

"No, thanks. Afterwards, perhaps," Bony decided.

Again Simpson smiled, although his eyes remained cold. He said:

"My mother isn't feeling very well today, so perhaps I could leave a bottle or two in your room?"

"Yes, that's an idea. You might let me have a bottle of whisky and some soda water. I'll be going to bed early."

Simpson nodded assent and then looked down at the old man, who had said not a word:

"Now then, Father, I'm putting you to bed before I dress."

"Don't wanta go to bed," shouted the invalid. "Too early. Hours yet to sundown."

20

"Well, you'll have to go," Simpson said sharply. "Ferris is dressing and Mum isn't so well. She won't want to be bothered with you after she's cleared up."

The son moved to the back of the chair and winked at Bony.

The father shouted that he could put himself to bed, that he needn't go to bed ever, that he could sleep in his chair anywhere and any time, that Bony could put him to bed later. Despite his protests, he was wheeled away round the far corner of the building, one frail hand thumping an arm rest, the mane of white hair tossing with rage. His voice became blanketed, and Bony guessed he had been taken into a room just beyond the corner of the building, but he could still hear the protests, which availed nothing. Then the old man's voice sank away into a murmur, and Bony thought it strange that not once had the son spoken after disappearing with the invalid.

The feeling of pity for old Simpson was being qualified by interest in him. Why would his son not allow him to talk to guests? He did not appear to be *non compos mentis*. Slightly senile, perhaps. Irritable and often desperately miserable, without doubt. Who would not be so when suffering from such ailments? He wanted merely to talk. And if a guest didn't mind putting up with him, why was he denied?

Was it because he was likely to divulge family matters to any stranger? Possibly. Almost any family is jealous of its cupboarded skeletons. To deny the old fellow drink was wise, but there could be another interpretation. A smile touched Bony's eyes. The subconscious had dictated to the conscious mind to order a bottle of whisky, when Bony seldom drank spirits. A dram might unloose a tongue to tell more of the spirit store and a body within.

The ethics would have to be determined later—if it became necessary, and that seemed doubtful. After all, an invalid who holds possession of property he is incapable of managing can be a martinet, and damaging grit in any business. The father a confirmed invalid, the son did have responsibilities in his mother and sister.

Simpson came round the corner of the veranda.

"Old boy never likes going to bed," he said. "Quite a trial

at times, and Mother has her work cut out, what with the cooking and all."

"Says he suffers from arthritis," observed Bony. "Very painful, isn't it?"

"Yes, that's so. Doctor says there's no hope of a cure. We give him a sleeping-tablet about ten." Simpson paused, pursed his lips, and gazed hard at Bony. "Don't like to ask you," he said. "Wouldn't if Mother was well. Ferris and I ought not to go to Dunkeld tonight, but—I wonder—would you mind slipping into the old boy's room about ten and giving him his tablet?"

"Not at all. Yes, I'll do that," assented Bony, and the not unattractive smile crept into the hard eyes and the over-fleshed face.

"I'll leave the tablet and the glass of water on the table in the hall. See that he doesn't spit out the tablet. He tries to sometimes. Been telling you all his troubles?"

"No," replied Bony. "No. He was relating to me how he and Mrs. Simpson first came here and settled down. Must have been hard going in those days, especially for a woman."

"Indeed, yes. Well, I must get out the car and then dress. I'll put the whisky and soda in your room and the old man's dope on the hall table. See you later. And thank you. Mother can get to bed as soon as dinner is cleared away. She'll be all right until Ferris comes home."

He moved briskly off the veranda, a man not in keeping with his environment. He was no backwoodsman, and Bony experienced bewilderment when relating him to the invalid. A car was being driven from the garage, and it was brought to the veranda steps. Simpson appeared again and passed into the building. After a little while Bony stood up and was able to see the car and gaze over the clearing, now shadowed from the westering sun.

It was a beautiful car, almost brand new, a Buick, all black and silver, dustless and gleaming. Bony recalled reading that the cost of these machines was more than eleven hundred pounds. Like Simpson, the car's environment wasn't right.

He was in the hall looking at the pictorial map of the locality when the dinner-gong was struck. The map had been drawn by an artist and was an ornament for any hallway. The hotel in the clearing was excellently depicted, and behind it were the yard buildings and a grassy paddock with stables and hen-houses, and beyond the paddock a vineyard. The track on which the Rolls had appeared was not drawn on the map farther back than the vineyard. The creek and the bridge carrying the road on to Lake George were pictured. All the details were clear. One could travel the road round to Lake George, and then onward in a rough curve to rejoin the road to Hall's Gap.

On entering the dining-room, Bony found a well-dressed couple seated at one of two set tables, and he received a little shock of astonishment when he recognised Simpson in an immaculate navy-blue double-breasted suit. His dinner companion was a girl well under thirty, equally well dressed. She rose to meet the guest and to indicate the other set table.

"Will you sit here, please?" she said, her voice low.

Bony bowed and sat down. He was offered the written menu and made his selection. He noted that the girl's hands were roughened by work and her make-up badly applied. She did not wear her clothes with the distinction her brother did his.

He was still waiting for his dinner when she and Simpson left their table and passed him on their way to the front entrance. Simpson walked with the grace of a trained man, preceding the girl and forgetful of holding open the swing door for her. Bony was reminded of an aboriginal woman following her lord and master.

A frail, aged woman entered the dining-room from the back, carrying a tray. Her straggly hair was white, she was grey of face, and her brown eyes were distinctly wistful. As she placed the soup before Bony she said in thin tones:

"You mustn't mind me waiting on you tonight. My daughter has gone to Dunkeld with her brother. She doesn't often have an evening out."

"Are you Mrs. Simpson?" Bony asked, rising.

"Yes," she replied, her eyes widening as she gazed up at him. "Now sit down and eat your soup. I think you'll like it. Do you like roast potatoes well done?"

He was drinking coffee when she said:

"I hope you won't feel lonely tonight. I'm going to bed early. I haven't been too well. Thank you for consenting to give my husband his tablet. He suffers dreadfully at times."

23

Again on his feet, for, despite this woman's work-a-day appearance and the fact that she was waiting upon him, there was that indefinable attribute in her personality which demanded respect. He said:

"You need have no concern for Mr. Simpson. I'll look after him. He's been telling me how you had to battle when first you settled here."

A smile lit the faded brown eyes, and the worn features caught the smile. Then, abruptly, the smile vanished.

"It wouldn't do to believe everything my husband says," she said. "He's very petulant. Those early years were hard, indeed. We both had to work and work. Then came the easier years, and I'm afraid my husband drank too much. Now he's paying for his sins. We all have to do that, you know. Now please excuse me, I have to get the yardman his dinner."

Bony sipped his coffee and smoked a cigarette. His mood was pensive. Man and woman had suffered hardships. They had worked and slaved and denied themselves to create a home in a wilderness. And Time had dogged them, worn away the youth and the strength, had given a little of joy and much of sorrow. These two, old Simpson and his wife! What had they achieved through hardship and toil and frugality? The one an emptiness—the other pain! They and their like had achieved a nation and saw not the splendour of it.

He sat on the veranda, watching the night steal across the clearing and listening to the birds going to roost. The son was reaping where the old folk had sown. How come that this small country hotel could afford smart clothes and an expensive car if the old people had not saved and scraped and denied themselves?

It was ten o'clock when he went to his room for the whisky. On his way out through the hall he picked up the glass of water and the tablet. The old man was awake, and he talked with him for ten minutes and managed to pass in through the bars a little comfort.

On the veranda the darkness was like scented velvet, and as he was about to pass under the bird-cage he directed his flash-light to it. The bird muttered, and he stooped and said softly:

"You and the old man are imprisoned for life, but he did have his fling."

CHAPTER IV

THE MAN FROM TEXAS

THE next morning Bony left the hotel as the sun was slipping above the summit of the rock-faced range. The sky was patterned by tiny puff clouds, and the wind played upon the strings of the scrub bordering the clearing. He crossed the little white bridge and strolled along the road to Lake George, and a white-haired terrier came racing after him. From beyond the hotel came the proud call of roosters, and within the bordering scrub bellbirds announced his passing.

Peace! Security! Tranquillity all-pervading! Certainly not an atmosphere of tragedy. Tragedy could, like an ogre, emerge from the creases of that face of granite and drop down silently upon those two girls, luring them off the road, luring them deep and deeper into the bush, herding them away from water and then snapping at their weary feet, to hunt them farther and farther from help, until help was no longer so frantically urgent.

They had come to this quiet and homely hotel, two girls in their early twenties. And then one morning, when the sun was not much higher than now, they had slipped their arms through the straps of their packs, had shaken hands with Simpson and his sister. Here, just beyond the bridge, they had turned and waved to the licensee and Ferris Simpson, who were standing on the veranda. Then they had walked round this bend, and lo! no longer were they within sight of those at the hotel. They had walked on, and then what? It was as though that mountain face, or another, had bent down and with its iron mouth had devoured them.

It was now March, and that had been in October. In early December had come a man who, throughout the first twenty years of his life, had lived among mountains higher and wilder even than these. He was a trained investigator, the product of a hard school, and he had had ideas of his own concerning the bush and its powers. Had he succeeded in lifting the cover-

25

let lying so heavily upon the scene of that vanishment? Had he found a sign and, finding it, had the discovery brought steel-jacketed bullets to his body? Bolt smelled blood beneath the coverlet when none other did. To date, Bony could not smell blood, and in this he experienced slight disappointment.

He examined his impressions. First take that of James Simpson. Because he kept himself nattily dressed and wore expensive clothes when he visited the town, because he owned an expensive car and raced horses, one could not automatically suspect he had done away with two young women. The sister was quiet and minus her brother's somewhat forceful character and certainly did not fit into a background of violence. As for her mother—as well to imagine the old lady capable of competing with Joe Louis. That Old Man Simpson was a wreck on the shore of life, that his mind was not so agile as once it had been, was all too evident.

These people could have no motive for murdering their guests and, therefore, none for murdering Detective Price. Price had paid his bill, stowed his baggage in his car, had got in behind the wheel and shut the door. Then for a little while Simpson had stood beside the car chatting with him, expressing the hope that he would come again, promising to send word if a clue was found concerning the fate of the two girls.

Price had taken the track from which the girls had vanished, this same track trodden by Bony. He had driven past the guest-house at Lake George. There the people had recognised his car as, on two previous occasions, he had run over to take lunch. On then for five miles to reach the Dunkeld–Hall's Gap Road, and on over the slightly dangerous cross-over and down into the valley, at the lower end of which was the tourist resort. He was approximately twenty-two miles from the hotel when he was found dead in his car.

The evidence pointed to the assumption that he had been shot at the place he was found. On the door beside the wheel were Simpson's finger-prints, left there when he chatted to Price. There were no other prints save those of the mechanic at Dunkeld, who had serviced the machine.

The picture of the hotel and its inhabitants was brilliantly clear. It bore, however, one small smudge placed upon it by old Simpson, a garrulous ancient, a trifle spiteful towards those who guarded him from the Thing which had wrecked his body and brought his mind to the very verge of collapse.

Was the smudge on the picture more significant than a fly-speck?

The old man had uttered words which could have meaning. He had said that he possessed a key to the spirit store, and he had invited Bony to raid the store with him, a proposal obviously the product of a weakened mind. Then he had said that if his will was discovered, the door of the spirit store would be left open for him, "so's I could get inside and drink and drink and drink and never come out no more. Then I'd be another body in that spirit store, all stiff and cold."

Bony was examining the smudge when he came to an opening through the scrub not fashioned by the elements. It was narrow and littered with tree debris and once had been a used track. He recalled the details of his own map, and hereabout would be the track turning off to Baden Park Station. The slight mystery of this track not being drawn on the pictorial map in the hotel hall was now solved. Those at Baden Park Station now used a track skirting the hotel and the vineyard at its rear. He turned and walked back, and his mind went back, too, to the smudge on the picture.

Old Simpson had complained that his son would not allow him to talk with visitors. The son's attitude was, doubtless, based on the desire to prevent his guests being bored, for it was understandable that guests would want to lounge on the veranda and not have the old man continually "ear-bashing" them. And so, when the house was filled with guests the old man was banished to the rear, where he had the solace of the yardman's company, an elderly man by the name of Ted O'Brien.

This Ted O'Brien had been employed as yardman at the time the two girls had disappeared. He was referred to in the Official Summary of the case. Old Simpson had said that O'Brien had been "sacked" on having been discovered drunk in the spirit store, and in this matter Bony had gained another step when, the previous evening, he had given the old man a small nip of whisky before his tablet. To his question as to when O'Brien had been dismissed, old Simpson had said it was early in November, which was after the period covered by the Official Summary.

Simpson was perfectly justified in getting rid of an employee who had gained entry to the spirit store and drunk himself insensible. The fact that old Simpson averred that O'Brien was too honest to do such a thing counted for very little in view of his mental condition, but that little could not be discarded, and O'Brien's subsequent movements would have to be established.

And old Simpson's confidence would have to be further strengthened.

On crossing the little bridge, Bony saw the splendid Buick outside the garage being washed by a tall young man arrayed in blue overalls. Nearing the car cleaner, he greeted him and was regarded by wide-spaced hazel eyes beneath a shock of unruly brown hair.

"Mornin', sir. Been takin' the air?"

The voice raised the straight dark brows of the man who seldom exhibited astonishment.

"American, eh?" he exclaimed.

"Yes, sir, I'm from the United States. I'm Glen Shannon, the yardman here."

"And from the South?"

"Texas, and I got a little bit of home right here under my hands."

"It's certainly a beautiful car," Bony agreed. "Have you been working here long?"

The man from Texas wrung out a cloth and continued drying the mirror-like surface.

"Since just after Christmas," he replied with that pleasing drawl which creates for foreigners visions of sunlight and galloping horses and two-gun men. "Good job. Nothing much to do and plenty of time to do it."

"You like Australia, do you?"

"I like this place, sir. Reminds me of home. Back home us kids never saw a stranger once in a month. My pa had a ranch, and somehow we were mighty interested in things around. You know, horses and cattle and the usual chores. Guess it was the war that made a difference. I joined the Army and my kid brothers went into the Navy. Then, after the war was over and I went back home, it didn't seem the same. It was me who had changed. So—here I am."

"You'll go back some day, I suppose?"

"Oh, sure! Some day. Pa said: 'Roll around, son. Roll the moss off you. Us Shannons never yet had moss attached to us for long.'" The hazel eyes gleamed good-humouredly when directed to Bony, and Shannon laughed softly before adding: "Pa never had any moss on him that I can recall. He was as bald as a billiard ball. What part of Australia do you come from?"

The trick he had of tossing his hair back from his forehead and the swift smile which seemed to leap into his eyes Bony found very engaging. His chin was firm and his body looked hard. That he was yet thirty was to be doubted.

"I own a small place in New South Wales," he said. "It's about three hundred and fifty miles north. I run sheep."

"A sheepherder, eh? That's interesting. We never had nuthin' to do with sheep. You got many?"

"Something like ten thousand," replied Bony.

"Ten thousand! Say, that's a lot. How many acres on your ranch?"

"A hundred thousand. As I told you, it's only a small run." Shannon turned to face Bony.

"A hundred—— You're not kiddin'? What's a big place?"

"Farther outback—well, anything from three-quarters to a million acres."

Bony described his mythical small place, its lay-out, the type of country. Having digested this information, Shannon said:

"Musta cost you a lot of money to build a boundary fence around all them hundred thousand acres."

"Before the war it was roughly about twenty-two pounds a mile."

"That all! How many barb wires?"

"None. My fences contain only five plain wires."

Shannon frowned and turned back to his work. Then:

"Don't they have higher fences than that in your part of the country?" he persisted.

"No. There's no necessity."

Shannon rubbed hard upon a fender, and without straightening up he said:

"What would they keep inside a fence eight feet high with

29

a barb wire every six inches up from the ground, and an out-ward over-arm lay of five barb wires?"

"The Japs, I should think," replied Bony, laughing. "Where is there such a fence?"

"I don't recall. A fella stayin' here a couple weeks back was tellin' me. You got good roads where you ranch?"

"Fairish. We have difficulty in getting about in motors after heavy rain. Our roads are earth tracks, you know."

"How would I get along in wet weather on a motor-cycle?"

"Quite well. D'you own a motor-bike?"

"Yes. It's inside the garage. What's the best time to see your part of Australia?"

Shannon was avid for information. When in the Army he had visited Melbourne and Sydney, and it appeared now that the only brake to his desire to travel about the continent was the petrol rationing. He questioned the necessity for it, and Bony agreed that it was being maintained merely to keep a lot of people in quite unnecessary jobs. He gave his quick and open friendly smile as a reward for Bony's information, and Bony went into the hotel for breakfast.

Bony had often felt the urge to visit America, and the desire was strong as he breakfasted alone in the dining-room, waited on by Mrs. Simpson. No one knew Australia better than he—its powerful allure, its pervading aura of antiquity. There were two things he wanted to see in America: Death Valley and the Grand Canyon. There were three things he wanted to do: to be the guest of an Indian chief, to fish for marlin off the California coast, and to meet the Chief of the Federal Bureau of Investigation.

He spent the day on the hotel veranda dreaming of these things and how he might wangle four months' leave to make the dreams come true. Late in the afternoon he strolled along the track on which had come that magnificent Rolls-Royce. The sun was striking full upon the face of granite towering towards the zenith, and up that face most experienced moun-taineers might have climbed. The granite was warmly coloured from dark grey to brilliant rouge.

The track he followed in meditative mood took him past the hotel and its rear buildings, past a ten-acre grass paddock, on the far side of which were stables and hen-houses and a piggery, and then past an extensive vineyard which had been permitted to return to a wilderness. Beyond the vineyard the track turned right to skirt the foot of the tree-and-scrub-massed slope of the range rising to the sheer granite face. The skirting creek also turned right, and shortly afterwards the track began gently to rise diagonally up the slope, proceeding to a white-painted set of gates barring the way.

The gates were netted and of tubular steel. They were locked by a heavy padlock and chain, and beyond them the track went on up the slope and could be seen continuing along the foot of the rock face. Standing at the gates, Bony could see that the netted and barb-topped five-foot fence extended to the left as far as the granite cliff. To the right it dipped downward in the direction of the creek, and because a line had been cleared through the scrub to build and maintain it, he followed it downward and with no little astonishment saw that it ended at the creek. It was merely a wing and could serve no purpose excepting that the creek itself was a barrier.

Instead of returning along the fence to the track, he made his way down the creek bank, at first having considerable difficulty in progressing. Now and then he could see the vineyard fence beyond the track he had followed, and when almost opposite the divisional fence between vineyard and open grass paddock he came to a path which skirted the creek and gave easy walking.

As always, the ground interested him. On this narrow, winding path beside the creek he observed the imprints of birds' feet, wallabies, a fox, at least two dogs, and, presently, the footmarks of a large man. They were the imprints of Glen Shannon's boots.

He had come more than once along the path from the hotel and then had left the path where grew several smooth-barrelled white gums between the creek and the track.

A mark on the trunk of one of these trees attracted Bony, and on reaching it he found that the mark was actually a number of small wounds from which the tree had bled. There were at least thirty such wounds to be encompassed by a circle having a diameter of twelve inches.

The tree had been used as a target. The weapons making the wounds had not been spears, neither had they been arrows.

31

That left knives. Glen Shannon had come here to practise knife-throwing, and that he was expert was all too obvious. He had thrown from a distance of twenty paces, and not one knife had sunk into the bark outside the imaginary circle, and not one knife had made impact against the tree save with its point.

CHAPTER V

A TERMINOLOGICAL
INEXACTITUDE

AT dinner that evening the Simpson family and the American yardman occupied the other table, old Simpson in place at the head and being accorded reasonably sympathetic treatment by his family. Afterwards Bony joined the invalid on the veranda.

"You don't smoke?" he said.

"They wouldn't let me after I caught the bed afire." The old man was beginning to cry, when they heard the sound of an approaching car. "It'll be the Bensons," he announced. "No time for 'em. The present man ain't like his father. His sister's stuck-up too."

The car glided to a halt and Simpson emerged from the hall and hurried down the steps. Bony, seated parallel with the creeper festooning the front of the veranda, gently parted the vines that he might see without having to stand. He was in time to observe the male passenger open the door and invite the licensee to enter the vehicle and occupy a drop seat with his back to the driver. The door was left open.

Mr. Carl Benson occupied the corner nearer to Bony and thus presented his face in profile. He was a well-conditioned man of perhaps forty-five, his hair grey and close-cut. His face was strong and, although at ease, he did not smile.

"More brass than the King," whispered old Simpson. "Don't know what he does with it. Ain't spent much these last two years. Uster entertain a lot. Uster have big parties over at Baden Park. Down at Portland he has a large boat, but they haven't used it much these last two years."

The licensee was doing the listening, occasionally nodding in agreement with what was being said. The woman beyond Benson stifled a yawn with a gloved hand. She would be, Bony thought, several years younger than her brother.

"Can't be broke," muttered the old man. "Sold twenty rams

33

for an average of nine hundred quid only the other day. Not like his father, who was a good friend to me. The father uster come in for a drink. Never passed by without coming in to see me and the old woman. You goin' to slip me a drink tonight?"

"What did you promise—last night?" countered Bony. Simpson was leaving the car. He closed the door and said something Bony could not overhear. Benson's face was turned now to Bony. It was a cold, quiet, strong face. For the first time he smiled frostily, and the licensee stood back and watched the machine until it vanished round the end of the building.

"What are the guest-house people like at Lake George?" Bony asked.

"Don't know much about 'em," replied the invalid, as Simpson came up the veranda and entered the hotel. "Lund and his wife's staying there longer than I thought they'd hang out. Pretty desolate over there. I give 'em six months, but they been there three years. Place was shut up for nigh on five years afore they went there."

"They didn't build the place then?" Bony pressed, although he knew the details of the guest-house occupiers.

"No fear, they didn't," replied the old man. "The present Benson's father built the house as a sort of fishing camp. Lund's only renting the place. Any chance of you sneaking me out half a bottle of whisky?"

Bony leaned forward and touched a palsied leg.

"Can your son fight?" he asked.

"He! He!" tittered old Simpson. "Can he fight! Can he hell and galoots. Uster be the champ of the Western District."

"Then I'm not sneaking you out half a bottle of whisky," Bony said with exaggerated solemnity. "I'll bet that Ted O'Brien didn't risk having his head knocked off."

The rheumy eyes opened wide and the voice was stronger.

"I'll lay you a bottle of whisky to nothing that Ted O'Brien risked it more'n once. Now! What about half a bottle to nothin'?"

"Then he deserved getting the sack."

"He didn't get the sack for that. He got it for finding the door of the spirit store open and getting drunk inside. Leastways, that's what Jim told me."

"Where's his home, d'you know?" asked Bony.

"He! He! He's at home when he's got his hat on. Never had no home. Got a sister living at Hamilton, but he never writ to her, never went to see her for years. Sound man, Ted was. Nothin' flash about him. Always done his work. He——" The tears rolled down into the whiskers. "He never come to say good-bye to me. They musta told him a lot of lies about me. Or they wouldn't let him come and say good-bye, knowing I'd kick up hell's delight."

"Did they tell you how he left, who took him to Dunkeld?"

"He went away like he come here three years afore," answered the invalid. "On his two feet, that's how he went away. Rolled up his swag and got—like I would if only I could get meself outa this ruddy chair."

"Tell me——" Bony began, when music swelled swiftly into ponderous volume, died away, came in again strong and clear. Bony at first thought it was the radio. Someone within was playing an organ, and not a cheap instrument, but one having an extraordinary range. The old man became still, appeared to shrink lower into his chair. The music continued. The organist was a master.

"Who is playing?" Bony asked.

The old man raised a shaking hand and with the back of it brushed away tears from eyes which appeared to be ever ready to shed them.

"Jim," he said. "That organ cost a thousand pounds. Benson give it to him years ago. He got it all the way from Germany. He got two. It was afore the war."

They lapsed into an appreciative silence, and presently Bony said:

"Your son can certainly play."

The old man brightened and tittered.

"Jim could always play something or other. His mother bought him a mouth-organ when he was a nipper, and one day when the present Benson's father was here he heard Jim playing it. So what did he do? I'll tell you. The next time his own son went off to college in Melbourne, he sent Jim with him. They was at college for years. When Jim left college he could play a piano. His mother got me to buy one. Jim could play wonnerful, and sing, too. Sing proper. Then this Benson got him the organ, and they imported a man from the city to show him how to play it. Oh, drat 'em!"

Ferris Simpson appeared.

"Don't forget to sneak me in a drink," whispered the old man.

"They'd hear me," Bony countered.

"No fear. They all camp at the back. Only me and you is in front. Well, what d'you want, Ferris? Can't you leave me be when Mr. Parkes is talking to me friendly-like?"

She came and looked down upon the invalid, and from him to Bony.

"It's seven o'clock, Father," she said with peculiar woodenness. "You know that Jim insists that you go to bed at seven. Now don't be difficult. Go along quietly."

She passed to the back of the wheel-chair and so failed to see her father wink at Bony and slide the tip of his tongue to and fro across his mouth. He began to voice objections as he was taken round the angle of the veranda to his room. His voice drifted into the organ notes, was defeated, leaving Bony to resume his chair and give himself to Jim Simpson's playing.

It was dark when Simpson stopped, and a moment later he joined Bony, slipping into a chair and lighting a cigarette. Bony said:

"You play remarkably well."

"Only thing I really like doing. Do you play anything?"

"I can get a tune out of a gum leaf," admitted Bony. "You've a fine organ."

"Yes. A modern German instrument. They can't be beaten in that line." The glow of the cigarette being smoked over-rapidly now and then illuminated the man's face. "I'd take a cinema job in the city were it not for the old people. Can't leave them, and they won't stand uprooting. Have you dependants?"

"A wife and three boys," replied Bony truthfully.

"I was born here, but I'm hoping I won't die here. How long have you lived on your property?"

"Took it over in 1930."

"Never been up into New South Wales. Have promised myself a good round trip when petrol's easier. You must do all right for juice."

"I have had to do a lot of wangling," Bony explained, adding with a soft laugh: "One has to wangle all the time these days. I've made a bit of money these last three seasons, but what's the use? I want to build myself a new homestead but can't get the materials. I want a new car, and I've got cash to splash on one, but I have to wait my turn. You were lucky to get your Buick."

"Matter of fact, I was," Simpson agreed. "Benson—he's the near-by Station owner—put in for a Buick two years ago, and then when he got it he decided to wait for a new Rolls, and so he sold the Buick to me—on good terms, of course. What kind of sheep do you run?"

"Corriedale origin," Bony replied without hesitation. "I introduced the McDonald strain to give extra wool length. Know anything about sheep?"

"Next to nothing. We get a few ration sheep from the Bensons now and then."

"How many do they run?"

"Very few compared with your flocks. The yardman was talking about your place. The sheep and the acreage seemed to astonish him. The Bensons, of course, own the Grampians strain."

"They breed the Grampians, do they!" Bony chuckled. "A fellow would have to be a millionaire to buy their rams. How big is their place?"

"Thirty thousand acres, and only half of that any good. Still, what country is good, *is* good." Simpson paused to light another cigarette. "The Bensons don't encourage visitors. Can't blame them, of course. They have to keep their breeding secrets. How far out of Balranald is your place?"

"From Balranald Post Office to my homestead it's eighteen miles. As I was telling the yardman, it's billiard-table flat compared with this place. Pardon me for gossiping about you to myself. Are you the Simpson who figured in searching for two lost girls?"

"That's so." Simpson eased himself in his chair and tossed the cigarette end over the rail. "They stayed here, and after they left to walk on to Lake George no one ever saw them again."

"Terrible country to be lost in," Bony asserted.

"You're saying the truth, John. Terrible country to find anything in too. Trick anyone not used to getting around in it. There's a gully west of here by a mile that's at least a mile deep. Goes down straight. Could never understand why they left the road.

"Looks like bad tracking country too."

" 'Tis so. Large patches of it covered with shingle, and larger patches that spongy they wouldn't retain an elephant's tracks beyond a couple of hours. Care about a drink?"

As Bony followed his host along the passage to the small lounge he decided that the information he had gained had little if any importance. He was, however, receiving the impression that Simpson was slightly on guard and more than a little interested in his guest. Simpson unlocked the "cupboard", a small room off the lounge permitted to stock liquors for bona-fide guests when the public bar had to be closed. A narrow ledge dropped into place across the doorway, and the men stood on either side and drank.

"My sister and I, and the men from Baden Park, rode all over the scenery," Simpson continued. "Never found a track or a sign of them. We think one of them must have slipped over into that gully I mentioned, and the other fell over when trying to locate her. No getting down there. Now don't you go getting lost."

"I don't think I would," Bony said casually. "And I don't think I'll risk it. Fill them up, and I'll go to bed."

In the Official Summary and in the statements signed by Simpson and others there had been no mention of that gully "more than a mile deep".

CHAPTER VI

THE WATCHERS

A WEEK at Baden Park Hotel produced little of concrete evidence concerning the fate of the two girl hikers, but much of psychological interest for a man adept in withdrawing himself to watch people on the stage of life.

Superficially the Simpsons comprised an ordinary hardworking family of not unusual beginnings. The old people had adventured, built a home, established themselves in a secure living, reared their children. The passing years had weakened them and strengthened the remaining son until they had become mere ghosts of the past.

The ghosts might whimper and whisper with, however, as much effect on James Simpson as the rain upon the granite face of the mountains. It availed old Simpson nothing to rebel against physical incapacity. His wife glanced over her shoulder at the guests who had come to paint the mountains and to study the botanical marvels and she looked with disfavour at the moderns who arrived in fast cars with fast women to drink as fast as possible.

Ferris was also a rebel, but she had nothing of the old man's fire and the old woman's patience. She hated the mountains and the people who came to carouse, but she was a prisoner of loyalty to her parents, who would have suffocated in a city's suburbs. That her brother was also a prisoner, Bony suspected, but failed to understand what captivated him. In consequence, James Simpson provided most of the interest.

Doubtless, he drank far too much when the hotel was full of his "flash guests", as described by the old man, but throughout the period of Bony's visit he drank with moderation. He was informed on current subjects, was passionately fond of music, was seldom careless in speech, and was self-controlled. What caused Bony to speculate was why such an isolated place as Baden Park Hotel could hold such a man?

There were moments when Bony had seen Simpson regarding him with cold calculation. There were moments when an icy barrier had been raised to thwart questions possibly thought to be too probing. The man was completely confident in himself. Proof of his vanity was forthcoming during the visit of a man and his wife lasting from late one afternoon until the following morning. The presence of a young and good-looking woman produced in Simpson unsuspected fires which went unnoticed by the husband. The observant Bony saw the threat to the woman and knew that was the reason for her desire to leave. She felt the sex menace in Simpson and feared it.

Like almost every vain man, Simpson was a liar. He had said that his theory of the vanishment of the two hikers was that they had fallen into a gully at least a mile deep and located a mile westward of the hotel. According to his father, there was no such gully, and Bony had checked that by exploring the country.

In his unobtrusive manner he had done much exploring, the objective being the re-creating of an event which took place five months previously. And by observation as well as the spoken word, he was sure that both Simpson and Glen Shannon were extremely interested in his activities.

It was now the fifteenth day of March, and on October twenty-second last two young women had left the hotel to walk the track to the Lake George guest-house. It was not likely that they had not left the hotel that morning, because Ferris Simpson had stated they had done so. Together with her brother, she had watched them until the bend in the track had taken them to itself. Simpson's statement, unsupported by his sister, could have been regarded with doubt.

What Bony had learned, and what was not contained in the statements, was that Ferris Simpson had been dressing her father when the two girls were about to depart, and that her brother had been insistent that she leave the old man to join him in farewelling the guests. After they had left, so all the statements agreed, Simpson had started on a repair job on the garage which had occupied him for the remainder of that day.

Bony had scouted along the track from the hotel to the guest-house. He had repeatedly left the track to explore the natural paths through the scrub. With the patience of his maternal forebears, he had hunted for signs imprinted on this page of the Book of the Bush five months before. His task was more difficult than that of the geologists who came to study these mountains and could say how they had been formed ages since.

Despite the passage of five months since the girl hikers had left the hotel, the lack of clues was becoming significant. Normally they must have left clues for such as Bonaparte to discover and so reconstruct their fate as geologists are able to reconstruct the formation of mountains. In his field Bonaparte was equally a scientist.

It was the afternoon of the eighth day of his stay at Baden Park Hotel. He had slipped away shortly after lunch when aware that Simpson and the yardman were repairing the pumping engine up the creek, and for the twentieth time he was examining the ground on either side of the track to Lake George. Today, as previously, he could find nothing and he was now convinced that the two girls had not become lost in the bush.

A possible lead to their fate might lie upon an area of small shingle over which the track passed about a mile from the hotel. Bony was approaching it now on the return walk to the hotel, his deep blue eyes ceaselessly alert.

On reaching the shingle, he sat down with his back to a boulder and rolled a cigarette. Where the shingle lay, nothing grew. A few feet to his front the track crossed the shingle, the motor traffic laying down twin ruts like the lines of a railroad track. Despite the successive weights passing along the ruts, they were barely two inches deep, so firm was the ground beneath.

At some time in the past a motor vehicle had been turned here. It had come from the hotel, had been driven off the track, backed across it, and then angled to run into the ruts and to be stopped just before it would pass on to the softer earth. The marks made by the turning were so faint that Bony had crossed and recrossed the area on several occasions before he sighted them, and so followed their story-telling curves.

According to the gathered statements and the Official Summary, no vehicle had passed the hotel during the visit of the hikers and the following two days and nights. When the two hikers left the hotel they passed out of sight round that first bend which was but a hundred yards or so from the watching

Simpsons on their veranda. They would walk on and pass that old turn-off to Baden Park Station marked on Bony's map and subsequently disused in favour of the track down by the hotel and its vineyard. Eventually they would arrive at this shingle area. Supposing that on that day they came to a halted motor vehicle facing towards the hotel? Supposing they were seized, assaulted, killed? Leave motive alone for the nonce. Concentrate on that picture five months old.

Well, having arrived at the waiting motor vehicle, nothing would have persuaded the girls voluntarily to enter it. It wasn't going their way—or had it been turned after they were kidnapped and thrust inside it? Bony was not sure about this, but inclined to believe the turn had been made before they arrived.

When people are struggling items become detached from them. The more severe the struggle, the greater the number of items. Buttons, hairpins, dress ornaments, and even hairs. The struggle would occur in the vicinity of the parked car, and that portion of the shingle area would now receive his concentrated attention.

Take another step. Assuming the girls had been assaulted at this place and either killed or abducted to be killed elsewhere, how had the car passed the hotel that day? Old Simpson, James Simpson and his sister, Mrs. Simpson and O'Brien, the yardman, all had stated that no car passed the hotel that day—or on either of the two following days and nights.

But what if the car was Simpson's Buick? That would not pass the hotel. In the minds of all those questioned would be the picture of a visitor's car, a passing tourist's car. It could be a car from Baden Park Station, and still the people at the hotel would answer in the negative: Did any car pass that day or the day after?

But it was silly to prognosticate further. It was not Simpson's car. Simpson was not in it, anyway. After the girls had left the hotel he was known to have worked about the place. Did he, however, know what waited on the track for the hikers? And, knowing, did he provide an alibi by insisting on his sister's leaving their father's dressing to stand with him and wave farewell to them? If only the evidence of a struggle could be found where the car had waited!

The air was heavy with eucalyptus. The dominating mountain watched. One could not get away from those grey-and-brown granite eyes. Even in the dense scrub they sought one out. The impression they created was strong with Bony when he rose and sauntered over the loose shingle. Most of the shingle comprised white quartz, a carpet of some two inches thick. The sunlight was reflected in snowy whiteness, causing his eyes to contract to mere pin-points. The hours passed, and square foot by square foot the carpet all about the position of the parked car was diligently examined.

A grey fantail came from nowhere to watch and chirp and dance. The ants were diverted by quartz chips being disturbed. Once a bull ant crouched back upon its hind legs and glared at the man with cold, agate-hard hate. The shadows lengthened, but the passing of time was shut out of the mind of this man whose patience could accomplish the finding of a needle in a haystack.

He did, indeed, make an interesting discovery. He found a splinter of pink quartz in which was embedded a tiny shot of gold. The splinter was dropped into a side pocket with the nonchalance of a boy finding a rusty pocket-knife. The fantail continued to dance and flirt. Twice it flew into the bordering scrub and danced on the boughs and gave the alarm to anyone not preoccupied with gazing upon shingle square foot by square foot.

Of no interest to the crouching Bonaparte was a nut discarded by a car or truck, a half-smoked cigarette upon which no rain had fallen and therefore had not lain there longer than eleven days, and the remains of a glass bottle which had certainly been there for several years.

A detective who has no luck is sooner or later returned to the uniformed branch and the street beat. For an instant Luck smiled at the implacable Bony.

Now gold embedded in quartz is a natural phenomenon, but rubies are not found amid quartz shingle. Deep between two pieces of quartz a crimson eye stared out at Bony. On moving his head the merest fraction it vanished. Then he saw it again. He stretched forth a hand and lifted the quartz guarding it.

It was a ruby, or a stone remarkably like one. The tips of Bony's long fingers went down to it. A man said:

"What the hell are you looking for?"

With the ruby, the fingers took up a piece of quartz, and the

43

hand became still. Bony looked up. On the track just off the shingle stood James Simpson. He had a double-barrelled shot-gun nestling in the crook of his arm.

Bony stood up and tossed away the piece of quartz, with the tip of one finger imprisoning the ruby against his palm.

"Gold," he said lightly. "Likely-looking quartz around here."

Simpson's lip lifted, and he came forward on to the shingle. The fantail almost alighted on his felt hat and then flew on to dance on a boulder.

"You must be an optimist," sneered the licensee, and there was something in his eyes akin to that in the eyes of the bull ant. Bony chuckled. He conveyed the ruby to a side pocket and took from it the splinter of quartz.

"What would you say that is?" he asked, proffering the quartz to Simpson.

Simpson thrust forward his left hand, his eyes as hard as those of the mountain. Then his gaze fell to the piece of pink stone, and the rigidity of his body subsided.

CHAPTER VII

PROSPECTING

WAITED upon by Ferris Simpson, Bony ate in meditative mood the excellently prepared dinner. At the other table old Simpson twice attempted to break into the general conversation and was pointedly ignored by his son, who talked with Glen Shannon of gold and its incidence in their respective countries.

Simpson was dressed in an old but well-pressed dinner-suit, and the starched collar and shirt cuffs emphasised the weather-darkened skin of face and hands. His brown hair, parted high up, lay close to his head, which added strength to the face when in profile.

The man's reaction to the gold-shot quartz had been slightly baffling, especially in view of the general knowledge of gold being now revealed in his conversation with the American yardman.

When returning to the hotel with Bony, he had asserted it to be a "floater" brought away from the range in the distant past by, probably, water from a cloudburst. He had never found gold in the district, and no one ever had. It was the strangest fluke that Bony had found it, and then had come the pressing questions: Had Bony prospected for gold? Where and when? Had he ever staked a claim? All questions which could have been intended to get farther into Bony's background.

Simpson had said he was out after rabbits for the table, but Bony saw by his tracks that he had stood for several minutes watching him before he spoke, and before that he had advanced spasmodically from a point where first he sighted him, advanced as though desiring to do so without being noticed.

Rabbits! No, not along that road. Along by the creek there were rabbits. There were rabbits in the abandoned vineyard. It appeared as though Simpson had been looking for him, which would indicate that he was suspicious.

Throughout the meal Detective Price tried to emerge from

the back of Bony's mind, being frustrated only by the interest in Simpson and his reactions. The old man was wheeled away in his chair by his daughter, out through the door leading to the hall and the front veranda, and when she returned she brought the coffee and Bony lit a cigarette. It was then that Price won.

In Bony's mind the death of Detective Price had for some time been disassociated from the mystery of the hikers, but in view of what he had discovered this afternoon it demanded reconsideration. If Price had been killed by some person or persons responsible for the vanishment of the hikers, whereabouts along the chain of his investigation had he discovered a clue, or a link, which had made him an acute danger to those responsible for the vanishment? The subject was like a dog's curly tail which, on being smoothed straight, swiftly returns to the curl.

The same thing followed when the supposition was raised that Price was murdered because he had discovered a vital clue leading to the discharged yardman, Ted O'Brien. Old Simpson was so sure that the man would not have departed without saying good-bye to him. Supposing O'Brien had seen something, or discovered something concerning the two girls, and had been effectively silenced, and then suppose Price had discovered something of the yardman's fate, and himself been effectively silenced? That appeared to be a more reasonable hypothesis than that Price had found such a clue to the fate of the girls as Bony had that afternoon discovered.

It was not a ruby but a brilliant which had had a setting. Neither of the girls had worn hats when they left Melbourne, and one, Mavis Sanky, had worn a hair-clip studded with ornamental ruby-red brilliants. Her companion had been wearing a similar ornament decorated with emerald brilliants. The setting of both ornaments was nine-carat gold, and therefore the ornaments were not cheap and the stones would not easily fall out.

Bony decided he was licensed to assume that his picture of the car waiting on the shingle area was authentic. There had been a struggle during which the hair-clip worn by Mavis Sanky had dropped from her head, had been trodden upon as it lay on the shingle, had been picked up minus that one brilliant which had dropped down between the pieces of quartz and remained unseen.

Had the persons concerned in the struggle retrieved the hair-clip before they drove off with their prisoners, or had it been found by either the old yardman or by Detective Price?

Assumptions only, but they were all that Bony had gained, and as he passed out of the dining-room, already evacuated by the others, he determined to press forward with his interrogation of old Simpson.

On the few occasions he had been able freely to talk with the old man he had been unable to elicit anything further to the remark about the body in the spirit store. Old Simpson was deeply cunning or slightly decayed mentally, in either case aggravatingly so, and Bony was given the impression that he was being bargained with. If he wanted information he'd have to buy it with a drink or two. And with this in his mind, he passed on to the front veranda and was ordered to:

"Get to hell outa here," by the cockatoo.

"Don't you take no notice of that ruddy fowl," snarled the old man. "Come on over here and have a talk before they dump me into me cot like a body into a coffin. Where you get that floater, eh? I can't make head nor tail of it the way Jim tells it."

Having settled himself near the invalid, Bony described the shingle area and proffered the quartz for examination. Old Simpson held it to the light and squinted at the golden speck.

"I know the place," he said. "Might be as Jim said about being washed down by a cloudburst. It'd have to be that. Ground ain't low enough to have been the bed of a river."

"The quartz might have worked up from a reef underneath the shingle," Bony suggested, and the old man nodded quick agreement. He said:

"Pity Ted O'Brien ain't here. He'd have an idea or two. He done a lot of prospectin' around Ballarat in the old days. How long you staying on?"

"Few days, I expect."

The weak eyes peered at Bony and then were directed along the veranda to the caged bird. Bony could almost see the mind working.

"You pull out tomorrer," the old man said, hope in his voice. "You go down to Hamilton and find Ted's sister and

47

from her find out where Ted is. Show him this bit of quartz. Back him with a grub-stake and arrange to go partners with him. I'd like to see Ted again."

"Perhaps O'Brien didn't go back to Hamilton."

"Perhaps he never did. I ain't sure. I'd like to be." The old man's voice sank to a whisper. "The winder behind me—is it open?"

Bony brought his gaze upward to pass swiftly across the window next to that of his bedroom. He shook his head and then crossed to his bedroom window and, sweeping aside the curtains beyond, leaned inward to take a box of matches from the dressing-table. The door was closed and the room was empty.

On resuming his chair, he said:

"What's on your mind?"

"A drink, that's what's on my mind. That and old Ted who uster talk to me. You try and find Ted and hear what he says about that piece of quartz. Don't you tell Jim about it, about findin' Ted. He's going over to Baden Park tonight. That'll be him getting out the car. He goes over there some nights to play the organ for 'em."

Bony leaned forward, saying:

"Who else have you asked to find O'Brien?"

That gave the old man a shock. The thin, warped hands clasped and unclasped. The expression in the watery blue eyes became cunning, and the answer in the negative was forceful.

"Did O'Brien do any prospecting about here?" Bony persisted.

"Yes, sometimes."

"I suppose he used to cart in the firewood?"

"Course. That's the yardman's job. What's firewood got to do with prospectin'?"

"Did he use the horse and dray for prospecting?"

"No, nor did he use airyplanes. He had two good legs, didn't he?"

"How far would he go out for firewood? Two miles?"

"Nuthin' like it. There's enough good wood within half a mile of the place." The voice became petulant. "You tryin' to lead me around?"

Bony nodded.

"Yes," he said. "I'm wondering why you are so anxious to find out what happened to Ted O'Brien."

"I told you. Me and Ted were friends. Jim hadn't no right to sack him just because he got into the spirit store."

"Where there was a body all cold and stiff, eh?"

The old man tittered, gasped, and glared at the laughing Bonaparte. Bony stood up and stretched and yawned; then, gazing down upon the wreck, he said softly:

"Would you like a little drink tonight?"

"Would a man dying of thirst like snow water? You—you bring me in a little nip tonight, eh?"

"I might."

The sunken mouth writhed and a shaking hand was lifted to still the tremor. Bony studied the watering eyes, observed the struggle going on. Desire, cupidity, mental instability seemed enthroned at the one time. Old Simpson was far from satisfied that the old yardman had actually left the hotel, and he had stated his unbelief in the excuse put forward for the man's discharge.

"You keep a secret?" Bony asked.

"I'm full of secrets," was the reply.

"All right. I'll let you in on a secret later tonight. What time does your son usually return home from Baden Park?"

"About—any time between three in the morning and daybreak."

"I'll come in and have a chat with you about midnight."

"You'll fetch a nip?"

Nodding, Bony left the old man to stand for a moment or two before the bird's cage and then to saunter down the steps and cross to the bridge spanning the little creek. The Buick was parked outside the garage. The sun was setting, and the face of the mountain was like the face of an Eastern woman—partially hidden by the yashmak of purple silk.

Abruptly the wanderlust was upon him. He wondered what lay beyond the mountain, and through him swept the urge to climb it and look. Without doubt, beyond the mountain would lie another valley, and beyond that another mountain range, poised, restrained from crashing forward; but up there upon the crest he would stand in colour, be bathed by it, gaze into the flaming sunset, and have nothing of desire save wings with which to fly into greater freedom.

49

Down in the hotel clearing, standing on the bridge and listening to the water music and the whispering voice of the sleepy birds, he felt as a dungeoned prisoner must feel on gazing upward through the wall slit at the open sky. He was not happy, for the week had been filled with frustrations. Then he remembered the ruby-red brilliant and the tracks of the hotel dray which made a record for two miles through the scrub to a huge pile of rock rubble fallen from the mountain face.

When the dusk was deep Jim Simpson issued from the side door of the hotel and slid backward into the driving seat of his car. He drove away past the building, past the paddock at its rear, along the track skirting the creek, and onward to Baden Park Station. The engine purr dwindled to become the song of a drowsy bee, and when the bee alighted Bony knew that the machine was halted before the locked gates on what Simpson had said was Baden Park boundary.

With his ears he could trace the progress of the car up the incline beyond the gates. So quiet and soft was the falling night, despite all the aids to subdue its sound, the humming of the "bee" continued to pour inward from the outer silence. He heard Simpson change to second gear, and then he saw the car's headlights, a golden sword pointing to the evening star, wavering, swerving to the left, and illuminating a cliff of granite. A moment later he watched a mountain gorge open to receive the sword into its heart and the car into its iron embrace.

Someone switched on the veranda light, and Bony left the bridge and sauntered past the garage to see the yardman standing between it and the hotel, standing on the track taken by the Buick and listening as Bony had been doing. In its ill-fitting clothes, the figure appeared like a fire-blackened tree-stump, for Shannon did not move as Bony went on to the veranda, walking silently as only his progenitors knew how to move.

"Been out for a walk?" asked Ferris Simpson, who was seated beside her father.

"Oh, just over to the bridge," Bony replied. "I've been watching the sunset colours on the mountain. I think I'll do a little exploring tomorrow. You know, find a way to the top. I could go by the road, only the gates are kept locked."

"Don't you go into Baden Park country," ordered old Simpson. "They don't like trespassers. Too many valuable sheep over there. You stay this side of them gates. And don't you go climbing that mountain, either. Bits of it is liable to come away any time."

The girl vented a peculiarly nervous laugh. Her face was in shadow, and when she stood up it was still so.

"Please don't attempt to climb up, Mr. Parkes," she said. "As Father says, it's very dangerous. And—and we don't want any more trouble."

"Trouble, Miss Simpson?"

"Yes, trouble," snorted the old man. "What with people getting bushed and others getting shot to death and others going away without saying a how d'y'do to anyone, we've had enough trouble without you breaking your neck climbing that ruddy mountain."

"Father! Don't speak to Mr. Parkes like that!" exclaimed the girl.

"I'll speak to him how I like and when I like."

"You'll go to bed, that's what you'll do. Just see what comes of letting you stay up too late. Don't you take any notice of him, Mr. Parkes."

"Go climbing mountains!" shouted the old man. "So you'd push me off to bed, would you, me girl? Well, you just wait. You wait till I'm dead. Then you'll see." He was whirled away along the veranda and round the corner, shouting and threatening, and Bony sank into a chair and wanted to chuckle, for only he had observed the red eyelid close in a wink.

CHAPTER VIII

QUESTIONS IN THE DARK

IT was midnight when Bony, wearing pyjamas and dressing-gown, slid over the sill of his bedroom window. The night was soft and silent. His feet bare, he stole along the veranda and round the house corner to the french windows of old Simpson's room. This was situated on the side of the house opposite the bar and the garage beyond it, but Bony was confident that even there he would be able to hear the Buick returning. The french windows were wide and, when inside the room, he switched on his flashlight to make sure that the furniture had not been moved since that night he had given the old man his sleeping-tablet.

There was a table beside the three-quarter bed, and Bony sat on the floor so that one leg of it should be a back-rest. Beyond the foot of the bed the windows presented an oblong of steel grey, the door being on the far side of the bed. Finger-tips touched his head, and on the bed there was movement. Then old Simpson said:

"Did you bring a drink along with you?"

"I said I would," Bony replied. "Don't speak so loudly."

"It's all right. Ferris and the old woman sleep back of the house. Never mind if I want anything. Give the old bloke a pill that'll put him to sleep and keep him quiet. He—he! I wouldn't have swallered that pill tonight for anything. Why, I might have been doped when you came. What you bring, eh?"

"Whisky. Like a spot?"

The fingers touched Bony's hair, clenched, tugged. Bony removed the hand, shifted position, caught the hand again, and put into it the small glass. Simpson gulped, sighed, lowered the glass.

"Fill 'er up," he whispered imploringly.

"Don't be greedy," Bony told him. "I've only the one glass.

You'll have your share, don't worry. You don't know who I am, do you?"

"Well, you're not the Prime Minister."

"No—I'm not the P.M.—yet."

"You never know. There's been less likely-looking men than you. But you look out. There's hard doers to be met with up in these mountains. There was a detective staying here some time back and he met some of 'em over by Hall's Gap, and they done him in."

"Who are they?"

"Who? How the hell do I know? Hall's Gap is twenty-five miles from here. Did you come here for anything special?"

"To find Ted O'Brien. I'm his nephew."

The old man did not speak for fully half a minute. Then he said:

"Ted's nephew, eh! From Hamilton! So Ted never went away to see his sister?"

"Not so far. I thought I'd try and track him up, and so decided I would start at the beginning, start right here. You're a little doubtful about him, aren't you? When he was sacked, how much money would he have?"

The question required time to answer.

"Wouldn't know for sure," came the reply. "About a hundred and fifty quid, I suppose. Ted never spent much. He never went to Dunkeld. Told me he was tipped pretty good, too. He might of had more'n a hundred and fifty."

"Who would be likely to rob him?"

"Rob him!" snorted the invalid. "No one here would rob him. Jim's got plenty of money. He wouldn't rob old Ted O'Brien."

"Then why was my uncle killed?" demanded Bony, and when the old man spoke there was a nervous tremor in his voice.

"I think 'cos he got to know too much. I—— What are you giving me? You make me say things what's not in my mind. You——"

"Cut the cackle," Bony said roughly. "Ted O'Brien's my uncle and your old cobber, remember. When he was put off, or just before he was put off, were there any hard doers staying here or drinking here?"

"No."

"What time of day was it when you saw him for the last time?"

"When he put me to bed that night."

"He put you to bed!"

"Yes. The old woman and Ferris were having a bit of a spell down at Port Fairy, and Jim had gone over to Baden Park. Seems like that after having put me to bed, Ted went into the spirit store and got himself drunk. Jim found him on the floor the next morning and sobered him and then sacked him. Ted went away without coming in to say good-bye."

"And when did Mrs. Simpson and Ferris return home?"

"Some time later. Two days. It might have been three. I don't recall."

"There was no one else here, no one doing the cooking?"

"No. Jim's a good cook. There wasn't no need of a cook."

"Then what makes you think that something happened to my uncle?"

" 'Cos he never came to say good-bye afore he left. What about a drink?"

"What makes you think that something happened to my uncle?" repeated Bony.

"I told you." The voice broke. "Here's me alying here for hours in the dark waiting for you, and now you won't give me a taste. No one cares about me. I'm a lump of wood to be dragged up and pushed around and shoved into bed. But time's a-coming. You wait. You wait till after I'm dead, and then you'll see. They don't know where me will is put. They don't know that."

Bony let him run down and then passed him a couple of swallows.

"D'you know what I think about that uncle of mine?" he suggested, and when asked what, he went on: "I have the idea that my uncle found out something concerning those two young women who were lost near here. Did he tell you anything?"

"He said he didn't believe they were bushed. That's all."

"He never told you why he didn't believe they were bushed?"

"No, he never said. But he knew something about 'em." The trembling hand in the dark came to touch Bony's hair, clutch it. "Perhaps that's why Ted went away and never come in to say good-bye. It might be that. I been thinking other things, but it might be that."

Bony gently removed the fingers from his hair and eased his position on the floor.

"You remember the detective who stayed here? Did he talk to you much?"

"No. They wouldn't let him. You just wait till after I'm——"

"How did they prevent him talking to you?"

"Kept me off the front veranda, like they always do when there's a few guests," replied the old man. "We had a chip a coupler times, that's all. Price, his name was. He done a lot of ridin' around, but he never found anything. Them women were taken all right. After they left here they altered their minds about going to Lake George, I reckon. There's a turn-off about a mile this side of Lake George. Runs away to the west. Could have taken it and met some hard doers with a truck."

"Then how would Ted O'Brien find out about them—all that way from here?" countered Bony.

"How? I don't know. Ted, he found out something. Told me he had."

"Did you tell Price about Ted telling you that?"

"Never had the chance. Wouldn't of if I had. Don't want no ruddy policemen messing about here. Been a respectable hotel ever since the present Benson's father got me the licence."

"Did you mention the matter to your wife, or to Jim, that my uncle reckoned he'd found out something about those young women?"

"No fear," came the swift reply. "I never tell them any-thing. They don't ever tell me anything. They think I'm a lump of wood, but you wait. How's the bottle?"

"That terrier doesn't bark much at night, does he?"

"No. Only if a fox is huntin' near the hen-houses."

"Must be a fox about tonight. Jim often go to Baden Park?"

"Now and then. Been friends with Carl Benson since they was boys."

"Why are those gates kept locked all the time?" Bony pressed, and when the old man asked what gates he referred to, he went on: "Those gates at the foot of the range—between the range and the creek."

"That's Baden Park boundary," answered the old man. "How's the bottle?"

"Might be the boundary-line, but the gates do not serve to keep anything in or keep anything out."

"Don't they, though," chuckled the old man. "They keep curious strangers out. They keep the hotel guests out. People staying here like to walk up beside the crick, and then they come to the gates that are kept locked and they don't go any farther. Benson don't like strangers wandering on his property. Don't blame him at all. Not with thousand-pound rams to be thieved."

"I can well believe that. Did you talk much to those hiking girls who stayed here?"

"Yes, I did so. They was a coupler nice young women. The Bensons liked 'em too. Jim took 'em over to Baden Park the night afore they left. I did hear that Cora Benson wanted 'em to stay. Anyway, they had a good time. Ferris went too. Jim played the piano and the young women sang. Ferris said they sang pretty good."

Something was clicking a warning in Bony's mind. Was there any significance in the omission from the Official Summary and the statements of the visit to Baden Park Station of the two girls? Probably not. He poured a little whisky into the glass and placed it in the groping hand of the man on the bed. He heard the faint sound of swallowing and the gentle sigh of ecstasy and then he was on his knees and leaning over the old man and whispering with his mouth close to the whiskered cheek.

"Don't speak. Pretend to be asleep."

Sliding back to the floor, he pocketed the glass and the bottle. The silence was material, a substance filling the room from floor to ceiling. Came into the silence the whisper of moving bedclothes, and then the regular breathing of a man asleep. Cunning old bird. Likely enough, he had in the past been surreptitiously inspected in the small hours.

It was outside the french windows, not beyond the closed door. Bony detected the small creak of the veranda board he had himself located. He went forward to lie prone on his chest, his body then being parallel with the bed, and able to see the oblong of the windows. Slowly he worked his feet under the bed, his legs, his body. Then his head was beneath it, and by lifting the valance he could again see the shape of the windows.

The oblong became a frame encompassing a human figure. The size of the figure magically grew larger so that the frame vanished into it. Soft illumination broke the darkness, and Bony saw a man's feet and trouser cuffs within inches of his face. Whoever he was, he was standing at the foot of the bed and directing the handkerchief-filtered beam of a flashlight at the old man. There was no sound. There had been no sound to break the silence other than the old man's breathing, and Bony marvelled at the soundless entry into the bedroom. There was no sound now other than the breathing, regular, slightly stertorous.

The light went out. The oblong frame appeared dimly again and showed the figure of the man for a fraction of time. The man had stepped beyond the french windows and had gone along the veranda, and so round the corner to the front—if he was not waiting just outside.

Bony waited a full minute before edging out from beneath the bed. Stealing to the windows, he glanced cautiously round each and searched the blackness of the veranda and the lighter darkness beyond. Satisfied that the visitor to old Simpson's bed was not near, he stole back to the old man.

"Who was that?" he whispered.

"Don't know for sure. Didn't open me eyes. Likely enough it was Jim. How's the bottle?"

"But the Buick hasn't come back. We'd have heard it."

"He—he! Jim's got brains, he has," asserted the invalid. "Got 'em from his father. Jim's a bit suspicious, so prob'ly he left the car at the Bensons' gates and walked here. He done it before."

"When was that, d'you remember?"

"Too right! It was about the time them gals disappeared. He was hopin' to catch Ted O'Brien givin' me a drink. Mistook the night, sort of. Ted and me was havin' a nip or two the night before."

"Was that when my uncle told you he thought the girls hadn't been bushed?"

"Yes, it were. Me throat's that dry and all. Yes, it was then.

57

We was havin' a nip or two, and Jim came in and catched Ted giving me a tot. Jim did perform. But it came out all right. He didn't sack Ted till weeks after, and that was for getting drunk in the spirit store."

"What did you mean about a body being in the store—all stiff and cold, you said."

"Nuthin'. It was a sort of dream I had. How's the bottle?"

Bony told the old man to lie quiet, and himself went to the french windows, was assured, returned to the bed.

"Tell me about that dream," he urged.

"You gimme a drink. I'm dry talkin'," countered the old man. Bony pondered, standing in the dark, a part of his mind seeking to register the sound of the returning Buick, another part wondering what reliance could be placed in the cunning old rascal pleading for another drink. The old man asked quaveringly:

"You still there?"

"Yes. I'm waiting for you to tell me about the body in the spirit store."

"There wasn't no body, I tell you. I dreamed it one night. The body I saw lying there cold and stiff was me."

"When did you dream it?"

"When? How the hell can I remember when? Gimme a drink, quick."

Bony's voice was like the tinkle of ice in a wineglass.

"When—or no drink," he said.

"Blast you," snarled the old man. "It was that night Ted O'Brien put me to bed. I was having me dream when a curlew or something screamed on the veranda or somewhere and woke me up. Why don't you gimme a drink?"

"It wouldn't be my uncle who screamed, would it?"

"What d'you want to frighten me for?" wailed the invalid, so loudly that Bony almost clapped a hand over his mouth. "All in the dark, too. And Jim sneakin' in here and all. Course it wasn't Ted. Ted was drunk in the spirit store. Jim found him there the next morning."

"Very well. Let that slide. One other thing, and you tell me true and I'll give you another tot. The next day, the day after you had that dream, what did Jim do?"

"What did he do!" slowly repeated the old man, and Bony believed he was genuinely stirring his memory. "Why, he

58

gimme me breakfast here in bed and he tells me he's sacking Ted because he got drunk in the spirit store. And then, all morning, he took the horse and dray and went out after firewood, what Ted was supposed to fetch and didn't. And then he dressed me and put me on the veranda and played the organ all afternoon. After that he gimme dinner in the diningroom. And after that he put me back to bed. *Now* gimme that drink."

Bony gave a further two swallows, retrieved the glass, told the old man to go to sleep, and left the room, walking without noise back to his bedroom window. He had been in his room only a minute when he heard the Buick returning. It was then seven minutes to two.

CHAPTER IX

"HARD DOERS"

EARLY the next day the wind came to thresh the trees of weak leaves and dead wood and to keep the small birds deep in the protection of the creek scrub. It made the morning so unpleasant that Bony elected to read the newspapers in the small lounge serviced by the "cupboard", where Simpson, looking in on him, suggested a drink.

"Good-oh!" he said when Bony declined. "Day to be inside, all right. I'll be about when you want a drink. Gold fever burned out yet?"

"Never had it," Bony replied lightly. "I haven't the sporting spirit. To be a prospector one must be a gambler."

"Agreed. Wool and booze are dead certs. Still, I like a flutter now and then." The cold grey eyes were steady, having in them no reflection of the smile widening the sensuous mouth. "I'm going to Dunkeld this afternoon. Anything you'd like brought out?"

"Yes, if you would," Bony said. "Bring me a packet of Dr. Nailor's Digestion Tablets. It'll cost three and six."

"Get indigestion, do you?"

"Sometimes, and then badly. Was up most of last night. In fact, I went for a walk in my dressing-gown. Must have walked almost to the Dunkeld Road junction. Didn't hear you come in."

"Oh, I got home about two. I'll make a note of those tablets. Be seeing you."

He left for Dunkeld shortly after three. The wind gave signs of petering out by sundown, and after tea, taken with old Simpson on the veranda, Bony strolled beside the creek as far as the locked gates barring the road to Baden Park Station. Lingering for a little while, he found the evidence proving that Simpson had coasted his car down from the mountain crossing, had walked to the hotel, and then had returned for the car. The slight suspicion that the visitor to old Simpson's room the previous night had been Glen Shannon was thereupon banished.

On leaving the gates, Bony parted with the track, walking through the bush for a mile or more along the foot of the range, to examine the country in the vicinity of a little mountain of rocks sundered from the range when the world was young. A tiny stream came down from the range to pass by the little mountain and go whispering softly through the luscious scrub. Near-by Bony came to the tracks of the hotel dray, tracks now several months old.

He found, too, fresh tracks of both Simpson and the American. He had twice visited this locality, and these fresh foot tracks provided the evidence that when last he had been this way he had been kept under observation. It was proof of what he had "felt", of what the birds had indicated to him. The behaviour of the licensee and his yardman in keeping a guest under observation when that guest was merely taking the air, was surely motivated by something much at variance with the fear that the guest would lose himself in the scrub.

The little mountain of rocks was surrounded by a clear space, and several months back the hotel dray had been driven almost to the edge of the clearing. From both old Simpson and the yardman, Bony had learned that the dray was used only for carting firewood, and that ample supplies of wood were to be had within a mile of the premises. The place was two miles from the hotel, and the dray tracks were old enough to coincide with the dismissal of Ted O'Brien.

On the first of his previous visits Bony had circled the little mountain of rocks and found a natural passageway winding into its heart and ending at an open space as large as a small-house-room. He had this place in mind as a base for future operations, and he did not on this occasion approach the rock mountain, in case Glen Shannon was observing him.

Bony could not fit the American into this picture. Shannon had entered Simpson's service long after Detective Price had stayed at the hotel. However, enquiries concerning him would have to be made: when he had entered the country, his former employers in Australia, if any, and so on. It was not uncommon for American ex-servicemen who had visited Australia during the war to return. Many were coming back to seize the opportunities they thought awaited them, or to renew wartime friendships.

As it had promised, the wind lay down before sunset; and, having dined, Bony was occupying the front veranda with only the cockatoo for company, when he heard a car approaching from Dunkeld. He expected it to be Simpson's Buick. It was a well-conditioned tourer containing three men.

By parting the veranda creeper he watched them leave the car to stand for a moment looking over the hotel front. The cockatoo told them to "get to hell out of it", and they came up the veranda steps to greet the bird, whilst one knocked upon the fly-wire door.

Ferris Simpson answered the summons. The man who had knocked asked for dinner and accommodation for the night, and the girl invited them inside.

The surface of the pool of memory was stirred by a thoughtfish deep in Bony's mind. It was only for an instant, because he began to wonder not who they were, but what they were. He was thus speculating when old Simpson called from his bedroom.

"Who was that?" demanded the old man.

"New guests," Bony replied, when standing beside the bed.

"New guests, eh? How many?"

"Three. Three men."

"What kind of men? What do they look like?"

"One could be a university lecturer. Another could be a gentleman pirate disguised in a lounge suit. The third could be Superman. I think they're staying for the night."

The watery eyes blinked, were hard, cunning. The old man said:

"I heard Ferris at the front door. Did she know any of them?"

"I don't think so. Are you expecting people you know?"

"Expectin' people! We can always expect 'em. From what you said, these don't sound like hard doers. Still, you keep your eye on 'em. And bring me in a drink later on. I wonder. Yes, I'm thinkin' . . . Been wonderin' why I was put to bed so early. Wasn't no reason I could tell of."

Bony had reached the french window when the invalid called him back.

"Did you hear what I said about bringin' me a drink?"

62

"Yes, I heard," Bony answered. "It will depend on circumstances. Your son might arrive home at any minute. However, we'll see."

"Good for you, young Parkes. I hope you find out about your uncle."

Again old Simpson called when Bony had reached the windows. "Tell you what," he said, his upper lip lifted in a leer, revealing a toothless gum. "You promise me, and in return I'll tell you something you don't know."

"Promise what?"

"Promise you'll bring me in a drink. You'll be able to keep it."

"Very well, I promise. Now what?"

"Jim won't be back till early tomorrow. He's gone farther than Dunkeld. He's gone to Portland, and that's a hundred miles away."

"Oh! What for?"

"That's all I'm telling. You promised that drink, mind."

Bony attempted to probe, but won nothing. In flashes the old man was cunning, concerned, loyal to his clan, fearful for himself, uneasy for Bony. It was difficult to winnow the wheat from the chaff: how much of what he said and suggested could be accepted and how much rejected. For Bony there was only the one weapon. He used it now.

"Tell me why your son has gone to Portland and I'll bring you a double drink."

"That's a deal. I don't know exactly why. I don't think Ferris or the old woman knows why. I heard 'em talking about Jim having to go to Portland to fix up about March twenty-eight. Seems like that day's important for something or other. I'd tell you if I knew what about. Don't you forget that double drink you promised. And you——"

The voice broke away into silence, and presently Bony said: "Well—go on."

"You promise me you'll come and say good-bye to me afore you leave. Then I'll know the rights of it."

"That'll be easy to promise."

From the dusk-draped bed came a soft chuckle.

"Mightn't be so easy. No, you mightn't find it so easy if you're lying all cold and stiff in the spirit store. Anyways, if

63

you don't come and say good-bye I'll be thinkin' things about you."

Probing again without result, Bony left the invalid and the hotel to saunter along the track to Dunkeld, his mind being teased by the possibility of any significance of March twenty-eighth and the visit of James Simpson to Portland this night. He might establish the significance, if any, by running down to Portland or getting Superintendent Bolt to send one of his men to make enquiries. He was feeling that the line of the investigation he was at present following should be altered and the case attacked from a different angle. The murder of Price and the suspicions of old Simpson concerning the dismissal of O'Brien were becoming red herrings, annoying to one who still wanted to concentrate on the disappearance of the two young women.

On his return to the hotel he found the three new guests at ease under the veranda light. Coming upon them suddenly when he had mounted the steps, his problem was pushed into the background by interest in these men.

"Been for a stroll?" asked the university lecturer, and, detecting unctuousness in the thin voice, Bony changed his guess for that of a parson. Of middle age, the man had the brow and the eyes of the intellectual.

Bony admitted he had been for a walk and sat down in the chair invitingly moved for him by the man with the long black moustache, whom he had dubbed a pirate. Of the three, Superman was the most expensively dressed.

"Been staying long?" enquired the pirate.

"A week," was Bony's reply, his face angled as he rolled a cigarette. Somewhere deep in his mind lurked memory of this man or another much like him. He asked with polite interest: "What are your plans?"

"Oh, we are going on tomorrow," smoothly replied the parson. "There's fishing at Lake George, so we understand. Have you been to Lake George?"

Bony took in the light blue eyes, the thin mouth, the uncreased features above the flare of the match held to the cigarette.

"Yes, I ran over there a couple of times," he said. "Very pretty place. The guest-house proprietor told me that the fish were biting well."

The pirate said, studying Bony:

"Might give the fishing a birl. Anything to drink at this Lake George?"

"No, you would have to take it with you."

"Then I'm not staying at Lake George," announced Superman with a voice that boomed. "I'll get too thirsty, and I don't sleep when I'm thirsty."

"You drink far too much," the parson told him. "You have a magnificent body, and you have not any kind of right to harm it with alcohol. Moderation in all things, Toby, has been the advice of scholars and preachers down through the ages."

"Quit preaching at me," pleaded Superman, and the pirate cut in placatingly with:

"Are you from Melbourne?"

"No," Bony replied. "I have a small station outside Balranald. Taking the first holiday since before the war."

"Balranald!" murmured the pirate, and he began to twirl the points of his moustache. "I've never been there. Wealthy town, I understand. Someone told me there used to be seventeen hotels in Balranald."

"Talking of pubs makes me feel queer," asserted Superman. "What about a drink?"

The pirate ceased his attention to his moustache and regarded the large man with brows slightly raised. And then it was that the figure lurking deep in Bony's mind stepped to the surface and made its bow. It bowed from the photographic print of Antonio Zeno, proprietor of gambling schools and suspected of being connected with the murder of a business rival. It stepped aside to permit another to present itself in the guise of the parson. This was Frank Edson, a con man who had, prior to the war, risen to international status and, when on business, always favoured clerical garb. Edson's last term of imprisonment had been in Canada.

There was certainly something akin to old Simpson's hard doers in these two men. Bony glanced at Superman, and Superman said through the still haze of tobacco smoke:

"I want a drink."

"I am too comfortable to move," murmured the parson, stretching his long legs, and the gentleman pirate impatiently said:

"So am I. If you want a drink, Toby, go and get one. Take two, take three, a dozen."

Superman frowned and his square jaw hardened. He opened his mouth to speak and was stopped by the unctuous voice of the parson.

"There is, my dear friend, a time to be born and a time to die; a time to rest and a time to labour; a time to eat and a time to drink."

"Hell!" said Superman, lurching to his feet to stand above them like the range towering above the hotel. "The time to drink is when you swallow. Come on! You can't expect a man to drink with the flies. Trouble with you fellers is that you're too correct and too careful with yourselves. You'd regret all the missed chances to drink if you got run over by a tram or something."

Viciously kicking the chair back from his legs, he stalked to the door and entered the building.

"Friend Toby is ever too impatient," indolently remarked the parson. "Nice fellow and all that, you know."

"Better go along in and join him, I suppose," grudgingly surrendered the pirate. "Else he'll get himself drunk too early in the evening. What about you, sir?"

"No, I don't think so," replied Bony. "In another hour, perhaps."

"Well, you'd better come along," the parson was advised, and he frowned and compressed his lips for an instant before saying: "Yes, I suppose we ought to keep an eye on Toby. Still, I hardly approve of deserting our new acquaintance. Alter your decision, sir, and join us. I can assure you, we are moderate in our minor sins."

Bony smiled and assented. It was the old, old story. And he was supposed to be a man of means.

CHAPTER X

SPANNERS IN MACHINERY

SUPERMAN had prevailed on Ferris Simpson to open the "cupboard", and now she was standing within, and the narrow serving ledge had been dropped across the doorway. Her face indicated petulance.

Superman brightened at the arrival of his friends and Bony and invited them to name their drinks. The parson and the pirate called for whisky, Bony and the big man choosing beer, and whilst the drinks were coming up the pirate offered expensive cigarettes. They stood at the cupboard ledge despite the inviting easy-chairs, and for the first half-hour the "shouting" was not consonant with moderation. They talked of the mountains, the hotel, the fishing at Lake George, and Bony began to wonder when the inevitable personal interest would come to the fore. The angling was expert, the acting of both the parson and the pirate superb. Superman only was his natural self. The fish was enjoying the situation, when:

"Can't get it out of my head that I've seen you before," remarked the pirate. "I'm Matthew Lawrence. What's your name?"

"Jack Parkes," replied Bony. "It's unlikely we've met before, because I haven't been away from home since '39. Too much to do and too little petrol to do it with."

"H'm! Strange. Might have been in Sydney some time."

"Every man falls into one of about ten classes or types," murmured the parson. "Thus it is that often we think we've met someone before. You mentioned, did you not, that you are a pastoralist?"

"That's so. Wool production is my living."

"Hell of a good living, too," said Superman, grinning down at Bony. "Better'n wrestling for a living, anyway. I'm Toby Lucas. Toby to my pals."

"Ah, the lies men tell!" mocked the parson. He ranged himself closer to Bony. "Look at him. Perfect physical specimen of Man. The idol of the crowd, especially the female portion of it. Receives four hundred pounds every time he steps into the ring. And steps out again at the end of an hour or thereabouts. Do you make four hundred pounds an hour?"

"Not much more than four hundred in a year," Bony admitted truthfully.

"Neither do I—after having been freed by the Income Tax people. Just imagine four hundred pounds per hour, about sixteen hundred dollars an hour, or, if you'd like to take it in francs, about a hundred and ninety thousand francs per hour, just to step into a ring and bow to the fans, and then put on a dashed good act of rough stuff with plenty of hate with a fellow who is a bosom friend. Look at this Toby Lucas. Take in the expensive suit, the silk shirt, the diamond-studded wrist-watch, the bulging inside coat pocket, where he keeps his gigantic wad."

"And then look at me, at my shabby clothes, at my flat pockets," pleaded the pirate.

"And also at me, my dear Jack," urged the parson. "Regard me, Cyril Loxton, a slave to capitalistic bosses who demand sixty hours a week for a miserable few pounds. You'd never guess how hard I have to work—and at what."

"You are, I think, connected with a religious organisation," Bony said, and the others laughed without restraint.

"My dear fellow, you are very wide of the mark," the parson asserted smilingly, and yet Bony detected the smirk of satisfaction. "I am a debt collector. I collect long outstanding debts owed to other people. I pursue debtors until they pay up, and after they have paid up and thus freed themselves of a load, they dislike me. And whatever guess you made about Matt, here, it also would be wrong."

Bony asked Ferris to fill the glasses and then stood back to examine the pirate, whilst swaying slightly upon his own feet. In the instant his gaze had been directed to the girl, he had noted that she was troubled rather than annoyed.

"Give me three tries," he suggested.

"Bet you don't hit the bull's-eye," struck in Superman, and Bony wondered why con men are so unoriginal in their methods. Then he was presented with a variation, for the pirate accepted the challenge on his behalf.

"Bet he does," said the pirate. "Bet a level pound."

"Do me," agreed Superman. "Now then, Jack, old pal, I'm backing you to lose and so gain me a quid."

Drunken gravity well assumed, Bony stepped by the parson to pay Ferris for the drinks she had set up. Without speaking she took his money. He saw her glancing at the others waiting behind him, passing swiftly over them. Then she was gazing at him as one wishing to impart a warning, but not daring to do so. That was all, and he was puzzled.

Gravely he proffered the filled glasses, took up his own, and proceeded to look over the pirate as a man does a horse.

"You're in some kind of business," he said thickly. "Wait. That's not a guess. First guess is that you're a restaurant proprietor."

The pirate shook his head.

"All right! Second guess is that you're a fruit merchant."

"Oi!" exclaimed Superman. "Still out. Leaves you one guess to win me that pound."

"Better have another drink before making the third try," the parson suggested. "Thank you, Miss Simpson. The same again. This is becoming interesting. I think I'll chance a little pound on Mr. Parkes. Take it, Toby?"

Superman said he would even as he watched Bony, a broad grin on his great square face and his eyes a trifle hard. Ferris waited for Bony's glass, and the parson urged him to "drink up". Bony, however, retained his glass as he swayed and with determined gravity continued to examine the pirate. The room became silent.

"Ready?" he asked. "Here's my third try. You"—and he smiled foolishly—"you are the proprietor of a gambling den, a real slap-up, posh gambling school in Melbourne. Right?"

The gentleman pirate stroked his moustache with the knuckle of a long forefinger, a speculative gleam in his black eyes. The parson's fine brows rose to arch over his grey eyes which were no longer mocking. He was about to speak when Superman exploded:

"Well, I'll be back-slammed!"

"I'm afraid you are quite wrong, Mr. Parkes, and therefore Mr. Lawrence and I have to settle with Toby." With a quick hand movement he produced a wallet, speaking now more quickly with the evident intention of convincing a semi-drunken man of being in error. "Toby, your pound. As usual you have the luck. Matt—pay up. We must be good losers. I did think Mr. Parkes would bring it off. He came very close to doing so. What a joke though! Matt Lawrence, two-up king and emperor of the baccarat-tables."

"I don't find it a joke," the pirate said frigidly, and Bony supported himself by placing a hand upon the pirate's arm as he said: "By the way, what do you do? How far out was I?"

"I am, Mr. Parkes, a dress designer."

Bony chuckled and admitted he would never have guessed that. Superman pressed a full glass into his free hand. For the nth time the parson tossed a humorous remark to Ferris Simpson—and failed to melt the expression of cold watchfulness. Memory of what old Simpson had said stirred within Bony's quite clear mind. The old man had wanted to know if Ferris knew these men. When she answered the front door neither her demeanour nor her voice betrayed recognition, and yet her attitude towards these new guests since she had been in the "cupboard" was such as to include the probability of a previous knowledge of them and their activities.

The next move came quickly and confirmed Bony's suspicion that the girl knew these men and suspected their real intention towards him. Had their objective been to relieve him of his money through one of a thousand confidence tricks, the suggestion which was now made would never have been put forward.

"Let's all go for a walk," the parson said. "No doubt we could prevail upon Miss Simpson to open the cupboard for a little while before we turn in. What d'you say, Mr. Parkes?"

Con men of the parson's calibre do not take semi-drunks into a dark lane to rob them, and owners of gambling schools of the standard run by the pirate were not satisfied with a few pounds in the wallet of a man who might survive the robbery to identify them. Robbery, therefore, was not their motive. Bony's interest in them swiftly increased.

"I don' wanna go out for a walk," he protested. "Been out all the afternoon. Gonna sit down here and watch you fellers get drunk. Make me laugh to see rollin' aroun' a wrestler, a debt-collector, and big-time baccarat shot. Shorry. Mean dress designer."

Gravely determined, he occupied one of the easy chairs, eased his back, and closed his eyes. The parson said:

"Let him be, gentlemen. I fear our friend is slightly over-come. Again, please, Miss Simpson."

The girl was not in the "cupboard". Eyebrows were raised. The pirate leaned elegantly against the wall. The wrestler rubbed the palm of one hand with the enormous thumb of the other, belched, distended his cheeks. The parson sat down.

"At least the cupboard hasn't been closed on us," he said, and leaned backwards with his head resting against his clasped hands. "Ah, here is Miss Simpson. We thought you had deserted us, Miss Simpson."

"I went out for a fresh drying-cloth," the girl said tartly. "If you don't want any more drinks, I think I'll go to bed."

The wrestler smirked and said that the evening was still an infant. They kept Ferris busy for another twenty minutes, when the big man was showing signs of being drunk. No such signs were evident in his companions. Ferris's attention was being given to filling the glasses when the watching Bony saw the parson wink at the wrestler, who then looked towards Bony and grinned.

"Friend Jack oughta have a drink. Mustn't let him sleep all his brains away."

He came towards the seated Bony, and the other two turned to watch him, their backs pressed hard against the drop counter and thus preventing the girl from looking through into the lounge. He almost staggered in his walk, and when he pushed a hand against Bony's chest the weight was enough to wake the Sphinx.

"Come on, ole feller. Have another drink with Toby."

"I've had enough," Bony told him, and then was lifted by one hand to his feet and almost carried by one hand across the lounge to the waiting comrades. A glass of beer was offered to him by the pirate, and the wrestler said something about black men being unable to take it. He was working himself into a rage, Bony strongly suspecting it to be all pretence and won-dering what the little scheme was about.

"That's enough of that talk, Toby," the parson said sharply.

"I talk as I like to a feller who refuses to drink with me," bellowed the wrestler, drawing himself up and digging his fists into his hips. "What's the matter with me that he won't drink when I ask him?"

"I think you had all better go to bed," Ferris said, to which the large man asserted he was not going to bed, that he was remaining as long as he liked, and that he wanted another drink.

Ferris Simpson closed the cupboard door on them, and that, it appeared, was the act for which they had engineered.

"Ah!" breathed the wrestler, thrusting his bullet head towards Bony. "Now that the lady has left us, I'm going to give you a lesson in the manly art of wrestling."

He advanced upon Bony like a railway engine towards a light-blinded jack-rabbit. Bony backed away, coldly sober, tensed, believing that he now understood the reason actuating the coming of these notorious men. He was convinced that none here knew for sure that he was a detective, and therefore he could not declare himself even though he was defenceless, the gun given him by Superintendent Bolt being in his bedroom.

He turned and sprang for the door—to find it closed and blocked by the parson. There was a tiny smile at the corner of the pirate's mouth and the black eyes gleamed with anticipation. The wrestler ceased to advance, turned aside, and calmly pushed a chair away and the table against the wall. All pretence of being drunk was discarded.

"Well, now, Jack Parkes, since you have asked me to demonstrate on you the Indian death lock—and these gentlemen are witness that you did—I will now oblige you. No doubt you will have to enter a hospital or a nursing home for a little while, due, of course, to my slight inebriation and thus misjudgment, but you did insult me and that will be my excuse. I shall apologise and be very sorry and visit you often, and my publicity man will have a picture taken of me at your bedside. Now come to Daddy."

With astonishing quickness he was upon Bony, and Bony was equally quick. He attempted quite successfully the French drop kick taught him by an expert. The kick rocked the wrestler, and had it been given by a man of his own weight he would have been dropped cold. He swore viciously, and the parson called:

"Well done! Very well done! Now, Toby, kindly get busy."

Bony backed, crouched to take the onslaught with an offensive and was savagely pushed from behind by the pirate. The push sent him out of balance into the wrestler's huge hands, and in an instant he was on his back and his legs were gathered up, twisted into the wrestler's legs, and the wrestler, grinning down at him, proceeded merely to hold him fast.

"Excellent, Toby," cried the parson. "Do be careful now. Our friend only requires a slight rest, not a broken back. Honour will then be satisfied."

Toby's body began to lift, Bony's legs locked behind his own. Up and up he went preparatory to flinging himself backwards and thus strain and wrench the ligaments and muscles of a man hopelessly unable to bear it. The other two came closer. They leaned over the prostrate Bony, still smiling gently, but with the joy of sadists flaming in their unwinking eyes. Something which glittered streaked between the face of the wrestler and the two heads, and from the wall came a sharp twanging sound. Three pairs of evil eyes rose from the victim's face to clash, to waver, to move to the wall in which throbbed the blade of a throwing knife.

"You guys better let up, sort of," came the soft drawling voice of Glen Shannon. "If you don't, well, I just can't miss."

Like actors on a slow-motion film, the heads of the four men turned from gazing at the quivering knife to see the American yardman standing inside the cupboard, the door of which was wide open. On the serving-shelf were laid symmetrically four throwing knives. Another was lying along the palm of Shannon's open hand. Shannon said, and menace was like metal in his voice:

"Easy now, wrestler. Untie yourself. Think of a knife buried into your stomach, handle and all. Don't you other guys so much as blink."

The wrestler cursed, lifted his upper lip in a wide snarl. Then he went about freeing Bony's legs and, strangely enough, in this situation, Bony noticed the lacerated place on the great chin made by the toe of his shoe.

He and the wrestler rose to their feet. The others stood up, watchful, silent, poised like snakes ready to strike. This silence was whole, solid, something of weight, broken a moment later by the banging of a distant door. Along the passage came the tread of heavy men. A gruff voice drifted inward from the

73

back of the premises. The knives vanished from the cupboard-door shelf. Shannon drew back, snatched up a drying-cloth. The parson and the wrestler turned slowly to face the door. Bony sighed, and his mouth widened into a narrow red slit. The door opened violently, and two large men entered.

"Licensing Police here," announced one of them.

CHAPTER XI

THE RAID

NAPOLEON BONAPARTE was finding it necessary to exert will-power to subdue temper. He had suffered injury to his dignity, and that was also a blow to his pride, which could not easily accept physical defeat at the hands even of a man like Toby Lucas, one of the world's greatest mat men. That he had come within an ace of suffering physical injury was of less significance.

He regained command of himself during the moments when the two plain-clothes policemen took in the room, the open cupboard and Shannon standing within it and polishing a glass, the four hotel guests.

The raid had been efficiently conducted. The police car had been stopped a mile away from the hotel, and on foot the crew had arrived to surround the hotel and simultaneously enter it at the front and the back.

Two more policemen came into the lounge, and one of these took command. Unobserved by Bony, Ferris Simpson had entered the cupboard, and the American had emerged into the lounge to stand nonchalantly chewing gum. The girl was asked to bring the register.

"You men staying here?" demanded the police leader, and, having received affirmative replies, he waited silently for the register.

Bony sat down, emotional reaction causing leg and arm muscles to throb and heart to pound. Breathing was now slightly easier, but his brilliant blue eyes were still dilated and noticeable in the dark face. The leader of the raiding party flashed him a keen look the instant before he accepted the register, snapped open the leaves to lay bare the last entries, and examined the page.

"Who is John Parkes?" he asked.

"I am," Bony admitted. "Address is Coonley Station, via Balranald."

"Huh!" grunted the leader, as though by force of long habit he did not believe a word of it. "Well, which of you is Cyril Loxton?"

The parson answered. He was standing beside the table upon which he was elegantly leaning one hand.

"Your name is not Loxton. Your name is Edson." The slight movement of those in the room was stilled by that harshly spoken objection. "Which is Matthew Lawrence?"

"That's me," replied the pirate. "That is my name."

"Not in Australia it isn't. Your name in Australia is Antonio Zeno. And your name—your real name—you know, the name at birth?"

"Toby Lucas," replied the wrestler. "And you can't argue about it."

"Good!" The policeman signed the book and returned it to Ferris, who had stood by tight-lipped and silent. "I like people who stand by their legal names. Saw you at the stadium a month ago. The wife barracked plenty for you. Thought I recognised you. Must say you're pretty good on the mat. Still, I don't think you'd put up much of a performance against four of us, so calm down. Now, what about you? You're not in the book."

"I'm the yardman and general man employed here," replied Shannon, without ceasing to chew.

"How long you been employed here?"

Shannon said he had been working at the hotel for close on three months, and then, to Bony's astonishment, for the senior man had not once appeared to look in that direction, he was asked about the knife sticking from the wall.

"I tossed it," he announced. "Was giving a demonstration how it's done."

The senior man now stared at the knife and then went back to the American.

"H'm! Pretty good, eh? Friendly demonstration, I suppose?

"Sure."

"Glad to hear it. Name is?"

"Name's Glen Shannon."

Ferris was brought into the range of the hard hazel eyes.

"That O.K., Miss Simpson?"

"Yes, that's correct, Sergeant."

76

"Good! Shannon, you clear out. Miss Ferris, lock the cupboard and retire." He waited until Ferris and the yardman had withdrawn, and then he addressed himself to Antonio Zeno, asking how he had arrived. Zeno said he had come in his own car and, when this question was put to Edson and Lucas, they admitted they had travelled with the pirate.

"Well, we must get along, gentlemen," proceeded the leader. "Parkes, I am going into your background in a minute. You, Edson, and Zeno, I'm taking back to Melbourne—for identification, you know. I have reason to think that the names you gave me were false."

The parson stepped forward.

"Now look here, Sergeant, we're not doing any harm. Came here for a short holiday. We're going on to Lake George tomorrow for the fishing."

"Not now you're not, Edson. Better cuff 'em."

There followed swift movement, and the pirate and the parson were joined with steel. The wrestler glowered and clenched his hands.

"You'd better come with us back to the city, Lucas," he was told.

"But you can't do that to me," expostulated Lucas.

"You'd be surprised. Go and pack your dunnage, and then get out to the cars and be ready to push off."

"But, look——"

"No buts—Lucas—else I charge you with consorting."

There was no beating down the ice-cold hazel eyes, and following only a slight hesitation the wrestler left with the others and three of the policemen. The door was closed and the sergeant said:

"Superintendent Bolt asked me to tell you he was becoming anxious about you, sir. Said he doesn't want to crowd in, and so he asked our branch to run the rule over this place and contact you. Someone's been making enquiries about you."

Bony's brows rose a fraction, but he made no comment. The sergeant proceeded:

"Yesterday morning a telegram was received at Balranald from A. B. Bertram of 101A, Collins Street, City, to the Agricultural Experts' Association, Balranald, asking whether a person named John Parkes lived in the district. Bertram is an indent agent in a rather big way of business. Further to this

77

enquiry, a man called at the Motor Registration Branch yesterday afternoon asking to be told the owner of a car registered number 107 ARO, which, you remember, is the number now on the Superintendent's car. He wasn't granted the information, and he was kept until a man could be put on to him. He was trailed to A. B. Bertram, and subsequently identified as Frank Edson, con man. Naturally Edson was kept under observation and was seen to leave Melbourne with another criminal named Zeno, in the company of Toby Lucas, the wrestler. The car was reported passing through Bacchus Marsh and, having taken the road to Skipton, was later reported by Dunkeld as heading this way."

"They were not permitted to know they were under observation?"

"No, sir. They'll accept this call by us as routine work."

"Good. That's important. You report to Superintendent Bolt what I am about to relate, and say that I stress the importance of not being interfered with until I call for assistance —if I have to." Bony related what had happened in that room. "I'd like those three men to be held for as long as possible, but not to be charged with the assault on me, because it is vital that I continue with the character of John Parkes. Tell the Superintendent that I'll communicate with him some time tomorrow.

"Also ask him to check up on the yardman here, Glen Shannon. I think Shannon has been in the country only a few months. Better make a written note of that and other matters."

"Righto, sir. And——"

"Simpson, the licensee, went down to Portland this afternoon. It's most important to know why. I think that the date March twenty-eighth has something to do with the journey. Then at the time the young women vanished in this country, there was a yardman here by the name of Edward O'Brien. He left under somewhat peculiar circumstances. He has a sister living at Hamilton. I want to know where he is now. Got that?"

"Er—yes, sir, that's clear."

"Constable Groves might give a lead on O'Brien. You could call on Groves when you pass through Dunkeld."

The sergeant nodded, snapped shut his notebook, and then

as he slipped it into an inside pocket regarded Bony thoughtfully.

"The Superintendent said he would feel much easier in his mind if you could arrange to communicate with the Station at Dunkeld at least once in every twenty-four hours."

"I don't think that would be possible," Bony said, frowning. "Anyway, I'll be talking to him most likely tomorrow afternoon. Where is the nearest District Headquarters?"

"At Ballarat, sir."

"Then tell Superintendent Bolt that if I have not reported at Ballarat by midnight tomorrow—you can make another raid."

"All right, sir. Is that all?"

"That's all, Sergeant. Thanks for calling. Er—I'm sorry you ordered the cupboard to be shut."

The big man grinned with an abruptness which was startling.

"I could order it to be opened, sir."

"Then do so. I am going to bed. You fellows have a long drive back to the city. I'll say good night."

"Good night, sir, and all the doings."

Bony passed along the passage to his room and switched on the light. As he undressed, with intent he passed his shadow across the drawn blind that the three men in custody waiting in the cars, and probably Glen Shannon, might know his decision to retire for the night. Then, having slipped on a dressing-gown, he pocketed the whisky bottle and soda-water, added a glass, put out the light, and noiselessly raised the blind and climbed over the sill to the veranda.

The veranda was dark, and in case someone switched on a light, he moved to the far corner, where he waited in the black shadow of a roof support massed with wistaria. He stood there for some time before witnessing the departure of the police car and the gamblers' sedan for Dunkeld and the city. It was then ten minutes to twelve.

He continued to lounge there, his eyes constantly on the alert and probing into the lighter shades of the night-masked scene for sign of human movement. For many minutes he could hear the noise of the departing cars, and it was not until the night was empty of all sound that the tension seeped from his mind and his body.

As silently as James Simpson had visited his father, Bony reached the old man's bed and leaned low over him.

"Awake?" he murmured.

"Well, I ain't climbing up the chimbley," softly snarled the invalid.

"I've been having an exciting evening. That's why I'm late."

"All right! You needn't give it to me in writin'. Did you bring me a taste?"

"I said I would," Bony expostulated, and sat down upon the bed. "I promised you a double drink—otherwise two little drinks. Here's the first."

He could hear the gulp and the flinch of the whisky drinker, and then felt the touch of the empty glass. Without comment he gave the invalid the second of the promised drinks and heard again the gulp and the flinching only after the old man had asked what the uproar had been about and "men tramping all over the ruddy place."

"The Licensing Police paid a call," Bony explained. "They arrested the three new guests."

"Oh! Did they so! Whaffor?"

"Giving wrong names. Being known criminals. At least two of them are criminals. The third was taken for consorting with criminals. He's a wrestler by the name of Toby Lucas. Know him?"

"Only in the papers. The other two—did you hear their right names?"

"Frank Edson and Antonio Zeno. Know them?"

"Never heard of 'em." The old man broke into soft chuckling. "They play up?" he asked.

"They went quiet enough. Sure you never heard those names before?"

"I ain't no liar—unless I want to be. You describe 'em again. Names don't mean anything."

Bony gave a detailed description of both men and still Simpson failed to identify them.

"Never been here before," asserted the old man. "You said Ferris didn't know them either."

"I'm not quite so sure about that."

"Ah! Not so sure, eh? Gimme a drink."

Bony complied with what was a command.

"How they get along with you, young Parkes?"

Bony related the details of the evening in the lounge, and when he concluded the old man remained silent save for his low, slightly rasping breathing. It was a full minute before he spoke. On no previous occasion had he appeared to be so normal.

"I don't know. It makes me think things, John Parkes," he said. "I been worryin' a lot lately, and I oughtn't to be worried at my age. I still got the old woman to think on, and the hotel and everything. Ferris wouldn't be too bad without Jim. If I knew a bit more I could order him out of the place for keeps. You better go. You better leave tomorrer."

"I was thinking of doing so."

"You get away and look for old Ted O'Brien. Tell him I sent you along. Find out if he's all right and why he left without saying a good-bye to me. He knows something, does Ted. Told me he did. You tell him I been worried a lot over how things are going on here."

"And you really don't know why your son went down to Portland today?"

The old man became petulant. "I told you about that," he said.

"So you did. Did you ever hear of a man named A. B. Bertram?"

"Gimme another little drink. It's good for the memory."

Bony retrieved the glass in the dark. He said nothing, guessed the measure, and passed the drink to the invalid.

"A. B. Bertram," repeated the old man. "Yes, I know him. He's stayed here more'n once. Bit of a German, I've always thought. Plays the fiddle. Uster play it with Jim playing on the organ. What's he done?"

CHAPTER XII

JIM SIMPSON'S DECISION

BONY heard the Buick returning a few minutes before four o'clock, the silent night admitting the sound in time to enable him to see, through the open window of his bedroom, the clearing illumined by its headlights a moment before it passed to the garages.

Simpson did not appear before or during breakfast and, feeling well satisfied with the world, Bony greeted the cockatoo, seated himself in an easy chair on the veranda, and rolled a cigarette.

The sky was cloudless and the sunshine even thus early was hot. The March flies were an annoyance, for they make no sound in flight and alight on the skin without betrayal, to suck more blood than a leech if given the time. They had not been so bad for a dozen years.

Recent developments had added a swift increase of interest in the disappearance of the two young women, and this, instead of making Bony desirous of prolonging his stay at Baden Park Hotel, firmed his intention of leaving that morning.

The chief objective was to establish the fate of the two young women, and he was not going to be side-tracked by the fate of Detective Price and that of O'Brien, excepting that through the fate of either or both of the men he could proceed to learn the fate of the women. Price was dead, but it was far from certain that the old yardman was dead, and equally as far from certain that the girls were dead, despite all the circumstances which had to be accepted.

He had, as it were, attacked the investigation into the disappearance of the two women by the front door. He was held in suspicion by Jim Simpson, who, with the assistance of Glen Shannon, kept him constantly under observation. There was but the one way to evade the attention of both the licensee and the yardman, and that was to attack the investigation through the back door.

Simpson suspected him of being other than he had announced himself to be. He knew the man A. B. Bertram, and it appeared obvious that he had communicated with Bertram, who, in turn, had communicated with Frank Edson. It was possible that Simpson had not gone to Portland at all, that he had merely got out of the way whilst the men sent by Bertram dealt with his mysterious guest.

The mysterious guest was to be got rid of from the hotel, and there had to be no tragedy to achieve this desire. A slight accident during a drunken quarrel, perhaps, but no more. A point of interest was if the desire to be rid of him was on account of what he might discover or on account of having him away from the hotel on March twenty-eighth. Another death in these Grampians would most certainly be followed by tremendous police activity.

Assuming that the two girl hikers had been murdered, assuming that O'Brien had been murdered because he had learned something of the fate of the two girls, assuming that Detective Price had been murdered because he knew something concerning the fate of the girls or of Yardman O'Brien, then the motive for killing the girls must be exceedingly powerful.

The picture of Baden Park Hotel was out of focus and unbalanced. Jim Simpson had no place in the hotel itself, a dead-end place, a dead-end career for a man who was nothing if not ambitious. Simpson's present yardman also had no place in the picture. Beneath the pleasant exterior of the man there was ruthlessness, and an unbalance of the man when set against the work he was doing, an unbalance equally sharp, as if a hotel chef should undertake to clean the boots.

Bony was lazing in his chair and thinking of Ferris Simpson, who, if she did not know any of the three men who had arrived the evening before, might well have known why they came, when abruptly the licensee appeared.

"I'd like you to move on," he said, without preamble. Bony expressed surprise. "I'm not saying your name isn't what you say it is or that you're not what you've given out to be, but what happened last night makes it clear that those crooks came here to do you over. They have something against you, and I'm not going to stand for any gang warfare in my house."

"But were I a crook, or connected with those fellows, the

83

police would have arrested me too," objected Bony. "As far as I understand it, the wrestler became cranky with drink. He might have done me an injury but for the timely intervention of your yardman, but that they came here for that purpose I have distinct doubts. Had I been sure on the point, I would have complained to the police."

"That you didn't complain to the police clinches my opinion," snapped the licensee. "I don't want any argument about it. I want you to leave."

Bony pretended hurt astonishment, and Simpson departed. On the face of it, the man was justified, but Bony was sure that his reaction was assumed to achieve the result not achieved by the three visitors the previous evening.

The reaction of Ferris Simpson was equally interesting. She was stripping his bed when he entered the room to pack his cases, in her eyes anger and about her mouth the stubbornness of the weak. She looked at Bony with a steadiness he liked.

"I'm sorry you have to go," she said, so loudly it was evident she wanted Simpson to hear. "My brother isn't acting reasonably, but he's the boss, and there it is."

Bony gave the merest hint of the bow which so illumined his charm to women.

"Thank you," he said gravely. "However, I appreciate your brother's position and in his place might reason as he does. After all, you know, it isn't nice to have people on the premises who are arrested on sight by the Licensing Police, when they chance to come. I've enjoyed my stay here very much."

The girl's mouth melted into a wistful smile and, without speaking, she snatched up the used bed linen and left. Bony packed his suitcases and carried them to the hall where Simpson stood behind the office counter and silently presented his account. Bony paid, thanked the man for the change, and proceeded through the front door to the veranda.

Old Simpson in his chair was there.

"Cheerio, Mr. Simpson!" Bony called to him. "I'm leaving this morning. All the best."

"Nuts!" murmured the cockatoo. "What abouta drink?"

"Good-bye to you," replied the invalid. "Hope you had a good time."

Bony was passing down the steps when the bird flapped its wings and raged:

"Get to hell outa here!"

The staid, the correct, the polite Inspector Bonaparte turned, gazed up at the bird, and actually vented a raspberry. It was not until he was in his car and driving across the clearing that he permitted the scowl to leave his face, the scowl assumed in case the licensee was watching him from within the building. A moment later the humour created by the cockatoo vanished before the thought that old Simpson's appearance on the veranda might have been timed to provide a witness of his departure.

Assuming that Detective Price had been murdered for what he had discovered in or near this Baden Park Hotel and had then been allowed to travel as far as a mile or two this side of Hall's Gap before being shot to death, the same person or persons might have decided to let him get away before they attempted to deal with him in like fashion. It was, however, unlikely that further violence would be attempted, as the licensee's objective to be rid of him appeared obvious.

Notwithstanding, Bony took no avoidable chances. He drove along the narrow track to its junction with the Dunkeld Road, his eyes alert for danger and the Superintendent's automatic on the seat at his side; and, having reached the better road, he drove at high speed all the way to Dunkeld. On four occasions after leaving Dunkeld he halted the car at places of concealment to ascertain whether he was being followed.

It was after three o'clock when he garaged the car and a few minutes to four when, having enjoyed a meal more substantial than afternoon tea, he entered the police station at Ballarat.

"The name is John Parkes," he told the policeman on duty at the public counter. The man's eyes narrowed and at once he raised the drop-flat, inviting the caller to pass through.

"Come this way, sir," he said, and conducted Bony to a room, occupied by the divisional chief.

"So you are Inspector Bonaparte. Very pleased to meet you from the personal angle. Headquarters seem a little anxious about you. Sit down. My name's Mulligan." They shook hands.

He looked like a Mulligan, too—large and square of face and cropped hair as black as that of his visitor. Beady black eyes were now twinkling. He called the policeman back and told him to contact Superintendent Bolt at Headquarters.

When the door had been closed he went on:

"I'm guessing you're down in the Gramps on business. Had orders to look you up if you didn't call in here before midnight. How's shop?"

Bony looked up from his cigarette-making and smiled.

"Slightly attractive," he said. "Nice holiday. Beautiful locality. Plenty of local interest. Beer quite good and the cooking excellent.

"The Super said—well, I'll not repeat it. By shop I meant your official assignment."

Bony blew out the match and with some deliberation placed it on the ash-tray.

"I know that, Mulligan," he said lightly. "Your question I've answered truthfully. Nothing of apparent consequence has broken so far. Were you down there on the investigation into the Price murder?"

"Yes. And before that on the disappearance of two female hikers."

"Do you think there is any connection?"

"I've never made up my mind about it. Have you?"

Bony was saved having to answer by the telephone. Mulligan took the call.

"Yes, sir. Mulligan here. Mr. Parkes has just called in. Very well, sir."

Bony accepted the instrument and heard the voice which had spoken so gravely in Melbourne, which had come floating after him on the road to Dunkeld.

"Good afternoon, Super."

" 'Day, Bony. How's things?"

"Going along nicely. Are you taking care of the three gentlemen who were escorted back to the city last night?"

"Great care, Bony. Great care. Two of 'em are stinking eggs, but we haven't anything very serious on 'em at the moment. Still, we have enough to hold 'em for a few days. The wrestler was merely a stooge. The tale was put over that you had run away with Edson's wife and he was persuaded to take it out on you. He'll keep quiet from now on."

"The tale is untrue, Super."

"Of course it is," shouted Bolt. "I would never believe that of you. You never struck me as being a wolf."

Bony winced, glared at Mulligan, spoke with deliberate clarity:

"I mean, sir, that the wrestler's tale of the tale he was told is wrong. From what slipped out, the wrestler acted on a quite different motive. Have you released him?"

"Had to. Nothing on him."

"All right. What of the man A. B. Bertram?"

"Be easy, old pal," said the now soothing voice in Bony's ear. "We've been waiting to see if the wrestler contacts Bertram. Nothing against Bertram, either. Been in the country over forty years. Sound in business and a man of substance. You any idea who asked him to make enquiries about you?"

"No. Have you?"

"Not a shred. We got a line on the yardman, Glen Shannon. Home address is in Texas. Was in a paratroop company when discharged from the U.S. Army. Came to Australia last December. Purpose was to meet friends and see the country. Was in Australia for period during military service."

"Oh! That doesn't tell me much," Bony complained. "Learned anything yet of the former yardman, Edward O'Brien?"

"First report by the man on that job received about an hour ago. O'Brien's sister at Hamilton didn't know he had left the Baden Park Hotel. She hadn't heard from him since last June. He seldom wrote. That's all so far. The senior officer at Portland went into the visit there made by Simpson. He knows Simpson, who has been down there several times during the last two years to go fishing with Mr. Carl Benson and friends. He didn't see Simpson yesterday afternoon or last night, and he offers the suggestion that Simpson's visit was in connection with Benson's launch, which he knows is to be made ready for sea towards the end of the month."

"Oh! Didn't mention any date, did he?"

"Yes, as a matter of fact, he did. Said the launch was to be ready for Benson and a party of six on Tuesday, March twenty-eighth. Simpson home when you left?"

"Yes. He returned about four."

"How did he react to the affair last night?"

"Told me to get out. Said I was a crook, too, and that he wasn't having any gang warfare in his pub."

"Getting a line on him, or anything?"

87

"Nothing out of the ordinary," Bony replied. "Still, I'm not quite satisfied. Likely enough it was he who contacted Bertram. They are musical friends, I believe. It seems that he didn't like me being around. I find him interesting."

"I'm finding you interesting too," growled Bolt. "Go on. What next?"

"I want you to speak to Inspector Mulligan in a minute and ask him to do for me what I intend to ask him to do. I'm going back to Baden Park Hotel but by a different route."

"Now you are being especially interesting. Go on, pal."

"That's all, I think."

The growl became menacing.

"Oh, is it!" objected Bolt. "Now let me tell you something. I'm not liking this business with you sunk up to your ears in it and cut off from communication. The fact that those men were sent after you is a bad sign. I don't like bad signs, and I'm telling you. You wait there at Ballarat for one of my men to work with you. I'll send him off at the toot. I don't want another Price bump-off on my records."

"Better one than two more. I can take care of myself. It's a job that only little me can finalise. When I see the light, if there's any light to see, I'll not take chances. I promise that, and you promise not to interfere."

"And if I don't?"

A smile spread over Bony's face.

"Then I go back to Brisbane and report for duty to my own chief."

"Hug! What a man! What a pal! What a splendid black-mailer! You run the guts out of my car yet?"

"Your car is in excellent condition despite the fact that it's old and won't do more than fifty-two miles per hour. Now, are you ready to talk to Inspector Mulligan?"

"S'pose so. You suck me dry, don't you, but I don't get the same chance at you. Gosh, I wish I had you on my staff."

"You'd soon tire of me, Super. Now so long. Have a word with Mulligan, please. And don't worry about me. I'll arrange about keeping in contact and all that."

When Mulligan replaced the instrument he told Bony he had been asked to do everything required of him—even to robbing a bank.

"I have always liked Superintendent Bolt," Bony said. "He

is one of those rare men who is never hesitant to accept responsibility. Now, first, I want your word you will not report to him my requests excepting under circumstances I will outline later on."

"But Superintendent Bolt will want to know," Mulligan objected.

"You will be protected by your word to me."

"Very well. You have it."

"Thank you. By the way, I mustn't forget. I want you to take charge of Bolt's car. I've left it at the Haymarket Garage. See that it's returned to him as soon as convenient, and remember that he loves that antique more than a youth would love a hundred-horse-power roadster.

"Well, now. I have tried to get into the disappearance of those two girl hikers by the front door, as it were. I've been staying at the Baden Park Hotel for more than a week, and, as a matter of fact, I've become interested in the people running the place. It's my intention to return and enter by the back door.

"I am convinced that there are distinct disadvantages in numbers, and so I shall proceed alone. I want you to drive me to a point near the junction of the Hall's Gap—Dunkeld road with the track to the hotel, and there set me down. I intend to live on the country as much as possible, to go in as a swagman, and mooch around without being seen or tracked. I must purchase suitable clothes and rations and a quart pot. And I would like to leave Ballarat by six tonight."

"I'll be ready. I can get a car."

"Thanks. Have you, or could you obtain, a pistol fitted with a silencer?"

That made Mulligan's eyes shoot wide open. Then almost sorrowfully he shook his head.

"Going to be like that, eh?" he murmured. "I can let you have an automatic."

"I have one, but I wanted something silent. Never mind." Bony produced the pistol given him by Bolt and laid it upon the table. "I want at least fifty cartridges for this weapon. One ought always to provide for misses."

CHAPTER XIII

BY THE BACK DOOR

VIEWED from the north, the Grampians are minus features of interest, presenting a seemingly low and flat-topped front. It is when nearing Hall's Gap from the Western Highway that these mountains grow swiftly impressive, and it is on entering the Gap that one is conscious of the success with which they have hidden their grandeur.

Mulligan, wearing sports clothes, drove a well-conditioned car through the small tourist resort of Hall's Gap. Beside him sat Detective-Inspector Bonaparte, no longer debonair, no longer tastefully clad. The riding-breeches were new, but the boots and leggings belonged to Mulligan's son, who was an enthusiastic hiker. The coat was slightly too large, having been bought from a second-hand dealer, whilst the khaki shirt beneath the coat was one of Mulligan's own and four sizes too large. On the rear seat rested a blanket-roll within a canvas sheet, and a gunny-sack containing food, tobacco and matches, and a couple of boxes of pistol cartridges.

When a little more than two miles south of Hall's Gap, Mulligan said:

"This is where Price was found. His car was beside the road and facing towards Hall's Gap. Half a mile back along the road to Hall's Gap there was at that time a large camp of road-workers. It was not until half-past nine in the morning that the first traveller came along and saw the dead man still seated behind the steering-wheel as though he had fallen asleep. He had been shot through the brain with a .32. The engine was switched off, and the car was in neutral gear. It could be that Price steered the car to the side of the road, switched off the engine, and foot-braked to a stop. And that immediately after the stop he was shot dead."

"Indicating that either he was signalled to stop or that he met and recognised someone," added Bony with faint interrogation in his voice.

"That's so," agreed Mulligan. "There were no finger-prints inside the car other than those of Price. According to Simpson, Price washed and polished the machine the day before he left. Outside the door nearer the driver were Simpson's finger-prints, and Simpson made no bones about admitting that on the morning Price left he had leaned against the door chatting with him.

"Price left Baden Park Hotel on the afternoon of December thirteenth. He was found dead here the following morning. There were two bullet-marks inside and at the back of the car, and the two bullets were located. Three shots at least had been fired."

"Any theory about that—of your own?"

"Yes. That the killer opened fire as he ran towards Price and didn't know that his first shot had killed him."

"Seems sound deduction. No one at the camp hear the shooting?"

"No one. The evening of December thirteenth was still and hot. The night was still and warm. We chose two different days of similar conditions to fire pistols here and have men at the camp. Our men at the camp heard the reports, but they were not loud enough to awaken the lightest sleeper, and during the early part of the evening there was an accordion band concert in progress. However, after the roadmen had gone to bed, one was taken ill and another sat up all night with him. Neither of them heard any shooting."

"Giving strength to the theory that Price was not shot just here."

"Or that the killer had a silencer fitted to his pistol."

"Price was armed, I understand."

"A .22 revolver. A mere toy. It was snugly buried among his dunnage in a suitcase. It was his private property."

Mulligan drove on, and Bony fell pensively silent. The sun went down and the crests of forbidding mountains lay in wait for them. Dusk was falling when the road turned sharply to the endless range, taking them up and over the crossing, twisting and turning but newly formed and dangerous to careless drivers. It skirted the granite face of a mountain against which a planet might crash and, apparently, be repulsed. When they reached the farther valley it was dark.

They came to a sign-post having but one arm, annnouncing that Lake George was five miles distant. Then, twenty minutes later, they crossed the long bridge and met the sign-post having three arms, one of which indicated the track to Baden Park Hotel. When a hundred yards beyond the sign-post and still on the road to Dunkeld, Bony asked Mulligan to stop and switch off his lights.

"On coming to that sign-post for the first time," Bony said, "I could smell nothing but the gums and the good sweet earth. I'm now smelling something in addition to nature's scent. My gift of intuition is informing me that something extraordinary is being hidden in these mountains. Therefore, I shall not under-estimate probable forces exerted against me.

"Be easy, my dear Mulligan, and tell the Super to be easy too. There is no practical way to establish regular communication with either yourself or Constable Groves at Dunkeld. Maybe I shall have to call for assistance, or deem it necessary for the hotel to be raided, or meet with a situation impossible of being dealt with by myself. Therefore, I would like you to be prepared, to have cars and men ready for instant dispatch into this area on receiving a call direct from me or through Groves.

"That'll be fixed. You're going to live tough all right. What about extra supplies and that sort of thing?"

"I've enough rations to keep me going for ten days. There are rabbits to be snared and nice fat hens to be requisitioned from the hotel's small farm. I'll live better than in the Outback, for there is water everywhere and the winter rains are still a month away. Now we'll part company. You return to Ballarat via Dunkeld, so that there will be no turning round to arouse the suspicion of anyone hearing the sound of the movement and wondering why. Let me out before you switch on your lights. Au revoir!"

"Cheerio, and the best of possible luck, old man. I'll be waiting to hear from you."

Bony opened the door, stood on the running-board, tossed his swag and gunny-sack into the scrub, and then jumped from the car into the scrub and thus avoided leaving his tracks on the roadside. He crouched beside his dunnage and was concealed when the car's headlights were switched on. He watched the machine growing smaller in the frame of its own lights, watched it until it disappeared round a bend in the road, and listened until the sound of it was overmastered by the frogs in a near-by stream.

He sat on his swag and smoked cigarettes whilst the quiet and balmy night caressed him like a woman wanting to wean him from all distraction. Only very gradually did the night subdue the elation of the hunter, the chill of the hunted, the warm thrilling of the adventurer. He was alone in strange and glamorous country, and the vibrant instincts of his mother's race would not wholly submit. Now he was cut off from men and was the close companion of the living earth, clothed with tree and scrub. He would have to pass over the living earth upon his two feet, not along plain and easy roads, but over gully and mountain, and through tangled scrub and treacherous swamp, the while trying to see round corners and himself never to be seen.

A transformation of himself was going on, and it was not the first time in his life nor the first time he noted it with incurious interest. It was similar to the transformation of Stevenson's Dr. Jekyll, although the opposing influences were not good and evil, but rather the complex and the primitive in man. The highly-civilised Inspector Bonaparte was retreating before the incoming primitive hunter. The dapper, suave, and almost pedantic product of modern education and social intercourse, which is but a veneer laid upon the ego of modern man, was now being melted away from this often tragic figure, in whom ever warred the influence of two races.

Hitherto, Bonaparte had not wholly surrendered himself to his mother's racial instincts, the great weapon of pride winning for himself the battle. He would not wholly surrender himself on this occasion, but he did give himself in part because of the conditions which would govern his life for the next days or weeks, and because of the probable forces with which he would have to contend.

His career as an investigator of violent crime had been unmarred by a single failure, and this was due much less to keen reasoning and keen observation, than to the inherited lust for the chase, bequeathed to him by a race of the greatest hunters the world has ever known, a race which has had to employ reason, patience, and unbreakable determination to gain sustenance in a country where food was ever hard to win.

Within the rhythm of the battle of instincts and influences going on within, there was born a note of discord, and the contestants fell apart and were quiet, that the alarm could gain ascendancy. The conscious mind became receptive and through the ears strove to detect what had struck the discordant note. Bony could hear the bullfrogs, the rustling of insects, the trees breathing the zephyrs. Into this orchestral symphony came the low booming of a bass drum, and after split-second hesitation Bony decided what it was. It was rock falling down the face of a mountain range.

Then he heard that which had given the alarm. From the general direction of the hotel came the sound of a motor-cycle. It was coming from the hotel and was being driven at the highest speed permitted by the track.

Bony backed off his swag farther into the scrub and lay down behind it. At this level the road and the bush beyond presented a black and featureless void, and it was a full minute before the right edge of the void paled with light. A few seconds later the motor-cyclist arrived at the road junction, rounded the bend, and came roaring to pass him. The back glow of the single headlight clearly revealed Glen Shannon.

The image of the road and the scrub, across which had flashed the machine, faded out. The night fought with the sound and slowly, slowly won. Bony waited and wondered. And then his mouth widened and his upper lip lifted in a hard and fixed grin, for from the hotel he heard the sound of an oncoming car.

The car stopped at the road junction, its lights illuminating the world of trees and scrub to Bony's right. Upon hands and knees, he crept to the edge of the road, where he was able to see the junction and the men who were examining the ground. There were four men, three of whom Bony had not previously seen. The fourth man was James Simpson.

The men conferred for a little while and then vanished behind the car's headlights. The car was driven forward and turned on the junction, and it was not Simpson's Buick. It disappeared down the side track leading to the hotel, and the sound of it proved that the speed on the return journey was much slower.

It seemed that the four men had come thus far to establish whether the American had taken the road to Dunkeld or that to Hall's Gap. The tracks of the motor-cycle on the dusty road would have decided the matter for them.

CHAPTER XIV

BIRD'S-EYE VIEWS

IN every city throughout the world men watch houses and note who enter into and issue from them. Men watch houses from busy sidewalks, from dark doorways, and often from houses opposite. For the first time Bony watched a house from a mountain-top.

A great volume of water had passed down the creek to skirt the Baden Park Hotel since that early night when Mulligan left him on the roadside, but not much had been added to the investigation into the disappearance of the two girls.

Entry by the back door into this scene, as he had described his intention, had been effected in the dark of night. He had carried his swag and essential equipment for five miles over country extraordinarily difficult in broad daylight, and before dawn had made his camp inside the little mountain of rocks sundered from the parent range.

For five days now he had maintained observation on the hotel, and had employed the early hours of daylight in scouting expeditions, which previously he had been unable to conduct without being observed.

Having discovered a way up the face of the range to the summit, he had selected for his observation post two huge granite boulders set upon the very lip of the precipice and appearing as though a child could push them over. Between the boulders lay dark shadows, and behind them the scrub provided concealment from any who might come up the mountain slope.

From this vantage point Bony was able to gaze to the far limits of the great amphitheatre, in which old Simpson had founded a home and reared his family. The forest carpet of rough pile appeared to be almost level. Actually it concealed swamp and water gutter and creek, steep slope and stony outcrop, barrier of tangled scrub. He could see a section of the white bridge near the road junction, and the indentation on the forest carpet marking the track from the junction to the hotel and then on for some distance towards Lake George.

Fifteen hundred feet below, and seemingly so near that it was possible to drop a pebble upon the roof, stood the Baden Park Hotel, red-roofed and cream-painted. Nearer to the watcher, the hen-houses and the stables appeared like so many silver matchboxes, and the hens in freedom like white and black pinheads upon light green velvet. Nearer still was the square of the deserted vineyard.

Throughout the days of his vigil he had seen nothing untoward in the lives of those down at the hotel. Ferris Simpson fed the hens morning and evening, and her brother looked after the dray horse and the gelding he had recently purchased. On one afternoon he had harnessed the bigger animal to the dray and brought in a load of wood and thereafter was seen cutting the wood at a saw bench. Bony never once sighted Glen Shannon, and no other man appeared to take the yardman's place in the hotel organisation.

His early-morning scouting expeditions were not quite so profitless. He found that the hotel's electric power was brought over the range from the Station homestead, and that a direct telephone line connected the two places. And that was all, save the addition that Glen Shannon had done a great deal of hiking both before and after his, Bony's, stay at the hotel.

Because on the afternoon of this fifth day he wanted to sleep, he pinched out the current cigarette and carefully preserved the end to leave no clue to himself, as well as to conserve precious tobacco. Then, ready to move, he stood for a minute to scrutinise the scrub back of the boulders.

People could become lost and die in this country. A man could wander through and through it seeking help and never finding it. And yet! Bony recalled the story told by two men constructing a fence in the bush, a dozen miles from the nearest road and a hundred from the nearest township. They had run out of meat, and one had taken a rifle and hunted two miles from camp, where he had shot a kangaroo. As he was skinning it a mounted policeman rode out of the scrub to charge him with having killed a kangaroo in the closed season.

It was like that here—and probably more so. Because the bush looked empty, felt empty, the odd chance of someone observing him had to be recognised and countered with the utmost caution. There had been three men with Simpson at the road junction, three men he had not seen during his stay at the hotel. They might have come from Baden Park Station: they might be three of the hard doers Old Man Simpson had spoken of. And to clinch the argument for caution, no one had heard the three shots fired at Detective Price. No one would have done so had the pistol been fitted with a silencer.

The summit of the range back from its precipitous face was almost flat, the slope becoming gradually steep as the land fell towards the valley in which was situated Baden Park Station. Along the upper portion of the mountain back, the trees were short and the scrub was low and sparse. As he proceeded down the back, Bony employed every artifice to reduce the number of his bootprints. To glue feathers to his naked feet with blood, as his maternal ancestors were wont to do to evade pursuit, was out of the question, and the next best method, wearing boots of sheepskin with the wool on the outside, was prohibited by the toughness of the minor shrubs and the sharpness of the granite chips.

Fortunately, opposition, if encountered, would be by white men and not aborigines.

Taking advantage of granite outcrops and large flakes of stone which had become surface "floaters" from a parent reef, Bony made his way diagonally down the mountain back, intending to reach the track from the hotel to the Station after it had crossed the summit. The birds were his allies who saw everything, who twittered at everything which moved.

Quite abruptly he looked out over the valley, a wide and luscious valley, ironed into the greensward of well-tended paddocks whereupon grew wide-spaced red gums, providing shelter for stock. Down the centre of the valley ran a wide creek, its water gleaming like silver, and the creek partially encircled a spacious white house surrounded by ornamental trees. Near-by was a great domed block, the observatory, which in turn was flanked by outbuildings and the shearing shed. It was the most beautiful pastoral property Bony had ever beheld.

Continuing diagonally down the slope, he came to the road from the hotel. He followed the road, keeping wide from it, visually examining the scene ahead and watching the birds, and so to the foot of the range, where he was confronted by a fence.

With his back to a tree and himself partially concealed by scrub, he studied this fence. It was eight feet high. Iron posts carried the wires between larger strainer posts set every thousand feet apart, and from the ground upward every six inches was a barbed wire strained to the tautness of a violin string. Set at an angle of forty-five degrees, iron arms reached outward to carry five barbed wires. It was impossible for anything on four legs to climb over or pass through, and even the rabbits were frustrated by wire-netting. Save with wire-cutters, a man could not conquer this fence.

This must be the fence which Shannon had had in mind.

The gate was to the right, and cautiously Bony moved closer to it. It was the same height and similarly constructed, being fitted with a peculiar lock, which had no keyhole and no bolts. Outside the gate stood a small hut or shelter shed, from which a telephone wire passed to the nearest pole, carrying a telephone power line from the homestead to the hotel. Fifty feet inside the gateway a narrow band of metal was inset into the roadway.

Bony had seen similar fences built round government experimental farms, but never such a one enclosing private property. The cost per mile must have been very high, but in this case was certainly an insurance against the theft of extremely valuable animals and breeding secrets.

He smoked three cigarettes before moving away from the tree to stand beside the road for a close-up view of the gate. Now he observed that it was electrically controlled and without doubt was controlled from the house. And then, as though to show him how the gate worked, into the background silence of the day entered the humming of a car engine.

He wasted not a second in gaining concealment within a clump of scrub.

Simpson's Buick came snaking down the road to be stopped before the gate. Simpson was alone. He left the car and entered the little hut, and the ringing of the telephone bell reached Bony. Simpson was inside less than thirty seconds, and on emerging he crossed to the car and entered it.

The gate slowly swung inward. Simpson drove through the gateway. The car must have passed over the strip of metal inset into the road, and the gate closed silently, excepting for the final soft metallic clang.

CHAPTER XV

CRACKS IN THE PICTURE

MASKED by the leafy green in which he had found concealment, Bony relaxed and made a cigarette by shredding his
collection of ends.

It was evident that the electrically powered gate was controlled from the distant homestead and that it had been
opened when Simpson had announced his arrival by telephone.
It was also evident that when wishing to leave the property
the weight of the car passing over the metal strip would open
the gate and keep it open long enough for the vehicle to pass
through.

Beyond the fence at this place the scrub had been thinned to
such an extent that the homestead could be seen without difficulty. Bony estimated the distance as being a fraction under
two miles, the road to it running straight and level and marked
at intervals by side posts, painted white. At this low elevation
he could see the red roofs of the buildings and the massed
ornamental trees forming an arboreal oasis on the plain of
the cultivated valley. Slightly higher than the trees rose the
domed roof of the observatory.

What he could see of Baden Park Station was of interest
to Bonaparte the traveller, but held little significance to Bony,
the investigator into the disappearance of two young women.
That James Simpson was a constant visitor to the homestead
was accounted for by his childhood association with Carl Benson, by his ability to play an organ, and by the friendly
association of their respective fathers.

The American yardman had certainly seen this fence, and it
was most likely that he had visited the homestead with Simpson. There was no significance in Shannon's visit to the homestead, although there was in the vagueness with which Shannon had spoken of fences in general, as though he shared a
secret and could not refrain from seeking further information
about a particular fence.

Bony was content with his own situation at the moment.

The shade cast by the scrub was cool and he had found a comfortable back-rest against a boulder. Curious to see how the gate did open to permit Simpson to pass from the property, he decided to wait—and fell asleep.

The flug-flug of horse-hooves awoke him to see, riding past him on the far side of the fence, a stockman. He was not markedly different from a thousand other men employed on pastoral properties, save that he was better dressed. Instead of slacks, he wore riding-breeches and leggings having a brilliant gloss, matching the brown boots. His open-necked shirt was of good quality, and the horse he bestrode caused Bony's eyes to sparkle. Not common with the thousand stockmen used for comparison, was a repeating rifle in a polished scabbard attached to the saddle, and when the rider dismounted at the gate and the horse moved round, Bony saw attached to the other side of the saddle a compact wire strainer and a pair of shears within a leather case.

The man was on normal duty riding the fence, inspecting it for defects, as men are employed on government vermin fences. He walked his horse to a tree beside the road and neck-roped it to the trunk, and then, producing tobacco and papers, he proceeded to manufacture a smoke. The sun still shone from a clear sky, and the late afternoon was restfully peaceful.

Like Br'er Rabbit, Bony remained snug in his little bower, although he did not have Br'er Rabbit's obvious reasons for cautiousness. The stockman was young and fair-haired, keen and probably intelligent, but Bony continued to lie low. There was an indefinable something about the rider which divorced him from all Outback stockmen, and, try as he would, Bony could not detect it.

Having smoked the cigarette, the rider made himself another. He did not draw close to the gate and he appeared to have no intention of hurrying to the homestead, where his fellows would now have knocked off for the day.

Bony heard and saw the returning Buick before he did. The road being straight and well surfaced, Simpson drove at a mile per minute, and when he stopped the car just before the metal road strip the rider raised his hand in a careless salute before passing behind the car and arriving at the driver's lowered window.

Simpson's face registered subsiding anger. The younger

man's face registered change from good humour to concern. What they said Bony could not hear, but it was evident to him that Simpson rapidly explained what had put him out and that the other listened with sympathy.

Thus a full minute passed, when the younger man stepped back and Simpson put the car into gear and moved it slowly over the metal strip. The gate began to open. The young man called loudly enough for Bony to hear:

"Don't envy you your job."

Simpson nodded that he had heard and drove through the gateway, the car leaped forward to take the mountain grade at a speed clearly indicative of the driver's mood. The gate clanged shut, and the rider rolled his third cigarette.

Ten to fifteen minutes passed, for Bony disturbed by a crow which was unpleasantly suspicious of the clump of scrub in which he lay, when he heard the approach of another horseman coming to the gate from the opposite direction. This second stockman was as nattily dressed as the first. He also bestrode a horse which made Bony's eyes light with admiration. Like the first, he had a rifle in its scabbard attached to the saddle. He was older, grey of hair, stolid and stern.

The younger man freed his horse and mounted. Again he raised his right hand in greeting and the other returned the salutation, before the horses came together and were walked at a smart pace along the road to the homestead. Then it was that Bony detected the indefinable difference with the common run of stockmen.

They rode not with the easy grace of stockmen, but with the stiffness of soldiers.

The picture of the luscious valley and the magnificent homestead, the fenced paddocks, divided by the well-kept road, the electrically controlled entrance gate and the efficient fence, and the two horsemen returning to their quarters, was somewhere not quite true to the Australian scene. In balance and proportion, yes. It was its atmosphere which was not truly authentic, and Bony was mystified and therefore troubled in mind.

He wondered how often the boundary fence was patrolled. He assumed that the two riders had left the homestead together to reach the fence on the far side of the homestead, and there to part and "ride the fence" to meet at the gate. It would certainly be uneconomic not to inspect such a fence regularly and maintain its high efficiency.

The sun said it was twenty minutes to six when Bony left the clump of scrub and made his careful way upward along the mountain slope, and on reaching the crest overlooking the hotel he sprawled for a little while behind a bush, watching the way he had come and the birds about him, to see if they had an interest in other than himself.

Not that he suspected having been trailed or observed at any time since leaving Inspector Mulligan. The country about the Baden Park Hotel and Lake George was uncultivated, unfenced, unstocked, but somewhere in its virgin close was the reason why Simpson had ordered him to leave. Somewhere beneath the carpet covering the great amphitheatre must be evidence proving the fate of two lost women, and Bony believed that it was the possible discovery of such evidence which had motivated the licensee.

The fiery sun was threatening the stilled waves of distant mountains as he made his way along the back of the range, his mind concentrated on the business of progressing without leaving tracks, and thus needing to choose firm granite slabs and tussock grass, which would almost immediately spring up again when his weight was removed.

He came to a wide crack in the face of the range, and down this crack he proceeded from ledge to ledge, to reach its shadowy bottom, and then down along its sharp decline to where it emerged at the base of the mountain face. Thereupon he needs must progress diagonally down the basic slope of the range in full view of anyone at the bottom, a risk he had to accept, for there was no other way within several miles.

His descent brought him behind the little mountain of rocks in which he had established his secret camp. The pile was at least two hundred feet in height and was composed of rocks, not one of which weighed less than a ton. The base was honeycombed with rough passages between the rocks, the passages, save one, being irregular in width and length. The one led to the very centre, and just before it ended there was a narrow branch passage giving entry to the cave which he had made his headquarters.

Gathering wood, he carried it to his retreat, his boots crunching upon the rock chips littering the passageway and then sinking a little into the sandy floor of the chamber. He made his fire between two boulders forming the walls and went out again with his billy and quart-pot for water. The sun was setting, and the little mountain and the great mountain face behind it were painted russet and purple. To his joy, he found a rabbit in one of his snares deep in the scrub beside the whispering stream.

Half an hour later the damper loaf was rising within its bed of hot ashes, and he was dining on bread baked the previous night and grilled rabbit, with milkless tea as the wine. He was a king in his palace, the bright-eyed rock lizards his courtiers, and, on the ramparts without, the changing of the guards— the night birds taking over duty from the day birds.

The cries of the guards without could not reach him in his granite chamber, were not strong enough to penetrate along the granite passages and down through the multi-shaped crevices through which entered the waning daylight. Although the chamber smelled dankly and the sand floor was damp, it was just pleasantly cool. Its massive solidity gave the feeling of restful safety to a man who, for fourteen hours, had striven to avoid the eyes of enemies.

When he had eaten, the light was cloister-dim. The little fire no longer produced flame, but the red ashes gave out comforting heat. It could not be thought that Bony had lost the art of squatting on his heels, his slim fingers being employed with paper and tobacco, for the balance was maintained with the ease of one who had not sat in a chair for many years. His gaze passed to the small heap of grey ash which the rising damper had cracked open and, through the cracks, was sending upwards spirals of steam having the delectable aroma of baking bread.

At some place outside the cave a stone clinked against another.

The brown fingers ceased movement, the body of the man solidifying into a bronze image of "A Stockman Taking His Ease". Stones do fall one upon another. Twice, once in the night and once in the day, Bony had heard the rumble of rocks crashing down a mountain face. The wearing elements leave rocks balanced precariously on ledge and point, and the moment must come when the wind and rain and the heat and cold will topple them over.

It was growing dark within the chamber when yet again a stone fell against another.

The precious cigarette was thrust into a side pocket. From the other side pocket came an automatic pistol. As a sleeping bullock will wake and with one action be in full stampede, so Bony rose from his heels and was in the passage outside the chamber, his back pressed against a rock, his head turned that his eyes could watch the perpendicular line of a corner.

A dingo! He doubted that it was, for a wild dog treads as lightly and as surely as a cat. It might be a rock wallaby. It might be a man. It might be merely the action of the falling temperature dislodging granite chips.

The light was going fast, being drawn upward through the granite sieve. The silence was a Thing roaring its menace into the brain of a man. Imagination was a weapon turned against him.

Was Imagination creating the slow-growing bulge on the line of that passage corner? Was Imagination creating with a granite chip and a sound a living Thing which skulked just beyond the corner, which . . . ? Was Imagination creating a steady glint of light at the corner line and at the height of a man's eyes?

Bony was like a plaster of pitch within the shallow crevice in the rock wall. The bulge seemed to grow upon the corner line, grow with the inevitability of a stalactite until at the end of a hundred thousand years the left side of a man was revealed.

With nerve-shattering swiftness the man came round the corner—to be frozen by the sight of two glittering eyes above the black shape of a pistol.

Not even in this situation was Bony's diction unusual. He said:

"Glen Shannon, I presume. Place your weapon on the floor and then support the roof."

The ex-hotel yardman sank down on bended knees, placed his pistol on the ground and stood up with his arms above his head.

"What's cookin'?" he asked, and Bony returned the only accurate answer:

"Bread."

CHAPTER XVI

SHANNON'S PLAY

As it would be infernally dark within a few minutes, the encounter was exceedingly inopportune. A man can easily be bailed up in daylight, or at night with the aid of a torch, but the limitation of eyesight is a fatal disadvantage in total darkness.

Ordering the American to step back, Bony in his turn sank on bended knees to retrieve Shannon's weapon, his eyes never leaving the man nor his pistol wavering. Even then he had with great reluctance to accept the probability that Shannon had a second weapon hidden in his clothes and the certainty that Shannon had somewhere on his person more than one throwing knife.

"This country owes your country a great debt," he said. "I should hate having to mark my personal recognition of it by shooting you. You must believe that, and also you must believe that, should you attempt a hostile act, I shall shoot to kill. Turn about and proceed to the outside entrance."

The American turned round, keeping his arms high. He said as he moved along the passage:

"I don't agree that you owe Uncle Sam much. It just happened that you Australians were somewhere in between Tojo's stern and Uncle Sam's boot. What do I do here—with my hands?"

"Lower them and go on. I'm right behind you—and I can still see."

"Hope you're not pointing the gun at my kidneys. I'd prefer it between the shoulder-blades."

"You have no choice. It will probably be in the back of the head—if you risk anything whatsoever."

One close behind the other, they emerged into the open and Shannon was ordered to sit with his back against a rock and his hands upon his knees. The evening still held light. He was without a hat and his fair hair was roughed and dry. His trousers from the knee down were badly slashed, denoting several days and nights in the bush. Recognition widened his mouth.

"I had an idea when I saw you at the shanty that you weren't just touring," he said. "Well, I guess it's your play."

"And I guess it's your play, Shannon. What are you doing here and why were you after me?"

"I wasn't after you—particularly. Didn't know you was you until this minute. Just happened to see you go in, and as you didn't come out, I decided I'd have to nail you for identification, sort of. Would have too, if I'd used my brain as Pa taught me to use it. I got myself up going round that corner of rock, making it so my gun hand came last. Say, what's your part in this script?"

"You are not clear to me, Shannon, and I don't want to have to take you for a long walk to Dunkeld," Bony said sharply. "Your intervention the other night when that wrestling fellow attacked me, although most welcome, does not square with your constant observation of my movements. There is another matter which puzzles me, and that is your hasty departure from the hotel. It's up to you to make yourself clear and to keep your hands firmly upon your knees."

"Well, you aren't at all clear to me, either. You might be a cop, but you don't talk like one. There'd be plenty of chances on the walk to Dunkeld. Seems we're both up a tree, don't it?"

There was no heat in the drawling voice and neither anger nor fear in the frank blue eyes, but beneath the voice and deep behind the eyes dwelt resolution which nothing would break. And then came decision to dissolve the stalemate, for he was convinced it was stalemate and that he was not unequally placed by Bony's wavering pistol.

"All right! I'll tell you," he said. "I'm looking for a pal of mine."

"Indeed! What is his name?"

"Her name is Mavis Sanky."

"Ah! Go on."

"She got herself lost in this country some time back. Queer country, too. I don't much like it. Been lost in it myself more'n once. There's no beginning or end to it. However, there is plenty of water running through it, and a fella has only to climb a mountain to find out where he happens to be. Funny thing about it is that my girl was used to the bush, her people being sheep owners."

Shannon's voice dwindled into the silent evening, and Bony's voice entered into it.

"What you say is all public property."

"Yes, I 'spect it is. But what isn't public property—yet—is that Mavis was my girl. We met in New Guinea. She was then in your Army. We planned to be married, but the war sort of took us apart. I wrote a couple or three times after I was sent on to the Marshalls. There I met a Jap and was a bit careless with him. He blew up and I was back in the States when I realised how silly it is to be careless with a Jap. I wrote a coupla times more to Mavis, and because she didn't write to me I got sore, not having sense enough to realise that wartime letters can take a year to go anywhere.

"The Army shipped me back home. Ma was sick. My kid brother was away with the Navy. The war stopped and Ma died. Pa took it badly, so did the sisters. Then one day nine letters came from Mavis, some of 'em written more'n a year before. I wanted to set about getting her over to the States so we could be married, and Pa had a spare ranch up his sleeve for me. However, Pa said to go and get her, as he reckoned it wasn't right to expect a girl to cross the world to reach me, what with floating mines and gov'ment restrictions and the rest, and because all the Shannons went after their women with their heads down and their boots on and didn't wait to be chased by 'em. Then Pa fell ill and sort of delayed things. Time I was ready to start, a letter came from Mavis's pa telling how she had been lost. Pa said to get going fast. So I came over by air."

"Another girl was with her, I understand," Bony said.

"Yes, that's so. Her name was Beryl Carson."

"After you arrived in Australia, did you contact the police?"

"No. After I had a talk with Mavis's pa I had the idea that if Mavis and her friend hadn't really been lost in the bush I wouldn't want the cops butting in. Are you a cop?"

"Assuming that your girl friend and her friend were not actually lost in the bush, that something quite different happened to them, what then?"

The American's face was a pale oval against the rock. It

was so dark that his eyes looked black. When he spoke the attractive drawl was absent.

"Pa always said never to spoil a private war by yelling for the cops."

Bony relaxed a trifle.

"Where have you left your swag?" he asked.

"Down the creek a bit. Say, *are* you a cop?"

Bony stood up, and without command Shannon rose with him.

"Not cop enough to spoil a private war."

He pocketed his pistol and proffered the other to its owner, saying:

"We will climb down out of that tree you spoke of. Get your swag and come to my camp. That bread will be baked too hard if it's not taken from the ashes."

He watched the tall, almost shambling figure merge into the black and featureless background of the scrub, confident that the American would return. He felt that Shannon knew much more about the Simpsons than he himself had learned, for Shannon had been employed at the hotel for several months and his tracks told of much activity. Then the figure appeared and advanced, carrying a hiker's pack from which dangled a quart-pot and a rabbit.

Without speaking Bony turned and entered the rough passage, groping forward in the darkness, the sound of boots on rock chips informing him of Shannon's presence behind him. At the short turn-off passage Shannon was told to wait. He saw a match being struck and flame mount from dry bark to feed on sticks that the Australian was placing one by one. When by invitation he entered the chamber, Bony was raking from the ashes his damper loaf.

"Where did you obtain that pistol—and the silencer fitted to it?" Bony asked, and Shannon set down his pack and sat on it.

"Fella in Melbourne sold me the gun for a hundred bucks. The silencer I bought from another fella who charged three hundred bucks. If I could bring a thousand pistols into this country I'd make a lot of money. The silencer isn't very efficient. Some day somebody's goin' to invent a real silencer, and then it's goin' to be bad for a lot of other guys and the cops. Can I cook a feed on your fire?"

"Of course. Get busy. Let me have your quart-pot and I'll take it with my billy to the creek. The firelight is safe enough. I've made sure of that. But we must talk softly because sound carries a long way and I don't wish to be located."

"By who?" Shannon asked, looking up from delving into his pack.

"The other side, of course. I find myself annoyed that you saw me this evening. I don't want to be further annoyed by gross carelessness."

"Pa used to say that carelessness made dead men. He was never careless, and he's still going strong."

Evidently Shannon's Pa had been tough, and Bony wondered about him and this son of his as he made his way to the creek where he washed before returning with the filled receptacles. The American spoke like an unsophisticated country boy, but there was plenty of sophistication about that silencer and those throwing knives.

Shannon had the pistol apart and was cleaning it with a rag.

"I got coffee," he said. "And a piece or two of grilled chicken. No bread, though. Can't get the knack of bakin' flapjacks on the coals. You show me some day?"

Bony promised that he would, noting the warmth in the pleasant voice and doubting no longer that the American's actions were truly motivated by his self-imposed mission. Shannon withdrew from the pack a paper parcel, opened it beside the fire to reveal what would be a chef's nightmare and which was described as grilled chicken. Observing Bony's frozen eyes, he grinned sheepishly, saying:

"Guess I'm no cook. Never had much of a chance to learn, what with Ma and the sisters to look after Pa and us kids. I can fry things in a pan and boil things in a can, but plain fire sort of frustrates me."

"I regret I cannot offer you a dinner," Bony said politely. "Had I known that you were calling, I would have saved a portion of my grilled rabbit. I can offer you, however, the remainder of yesterday's bread to assist you to eat that—er—"

"Fowl. One of Simpson's. Thanks for the bread. Pa used to say that a real man's grub should always be plain steak just singed and washed down with likker. The likker sort of loosens up the steak fibres in the stomach, and that's very good for the eyesight."

Bony brewed tea for them both and pensively smoked whilst the American ate ravenously. Now and then he caught Shannon looking at him with steady calculation. The tension was still in the boy; suspicion was still alive despite the acts of obvious friendship. The return of his pistol placed him at a disadvantage in this little game of wits, and he was feeling it.

"Scoop a hole in the sand and bury the bones," Bony said. They were squatted before the fire in the space between wall boulders, and Shannon cast a swift glance over his shoulder, then grinned and nodded, and with a hand made a hole and covered over the cleaned chicken bones. A little later Bony brought his swag and set it on the ground farther back from the fire and himself sat with the swag as a back-rest.

Shannon lit a cigarette with a fire stick and turned his body slightly so that he could face the detective-inspector.

"Well, do we begin?" he asked.

"Yes, if you're ready," Bony agreed. "I think our best course is to join forces. If we can agree to do that, then the next good thing to do would be for both to lay all his cards face up."

"Depends on how much of a cop you are. Suppose you tell me about that."

"Being a cop, suppose you tell me more of yourself. I am an officer of the law in this country. You are an alien and, moreover, in possession of a concealable weapon which is unregistered and for which you have not a licence. And in addition, your remarks about conducting a private war indicate your intention, in the near future, of committing a breach of the peace. How was it that you obtained employment at the hotel?"

"That's easy. I was stayin' over at Dunkeld and was havin' a few drinks with a couple of fellas when in came James Simpson. One of the others said I was wantin' work, and Simpson looked me over, asked a few questions, and then offered me the job of yardman and general man. Suited me."

"And how did you come to leave the hotel—in such a hurry?"

Shannon grinned and dropped another stick on to the fire.

"Perhaps for the same reason that you did," he replied. "Simpson said he didn't want me any more as there weren't any guests coming till Easter. I reckon he wasn't too pleased about me stopping that guy from twisting you inside out. Said he didn't approve of knife-throwing in his saloon. Told you to go too, didn't he?"

"How do you know that?"

"Ferris told me. I got along all right with Ferris. She knew something was doing that night, and she slipped out of the cupboard to have me at hand. She reckons that not everything in the garden is lovely, the ugliest thing being her brother."

"So she knew those men, eh?"

"Yes, she knew 'em, or rather two of 'em. I knew 'em, too, when I saw them, and that was when I was in the cupboard, Ferris having called me in. Those two guys, not the wrestler, came to the saloon six or seven weeks back. They insulted a woman who was staying, an artist woman. Used to get around a lot. Too much for Simpson, looks like. That night, as well, Simpson was out of the way, and the next morning when the woman complained to him he told her to go, saying he'd heard a different story. Seems like those guys are Simpson's plug-uglies. Question I ask myself is what Simpson has to hide that he don't like women artists and sheepmen on holiday poking around. Answer is, my girl and her pal. What you think?"

"I am not yet thinking that far," Bony answered. "Why were you so interested in my movements that you kept me under observation?"

"That's easy too. I wasn't keeping you under observation so much as I was keeping Simpson under observation because he was keeping you under observation. By then I had been getting around some myself. I'd gathered lots of impressions, if you know what I mean. Pa used to tell me before you start in on a guy it's best to have the feel of his background, and when you came to the saloon I'd got Simpson's background pretty well lined up."

"And you think that Simpson has something to hide?"

"He's got something so rotten to keep hidden that one day he came very near to attempting to shoot you. It was the day you found that bit of quartz with the gold in it. He was watching you for some time before he spoke. Once he half aimed the shot-gun at you and almost made me wing him with a knife."

Bony sighed. "It seems that you have had to keep me safe from several evils," he said. "Thank you, Shannon."

"That's all right, Mr.—say—Parkes—which will do until you tell me your right name. You see, keeping an eye on characters comes sorta easy to me, what with Pa's training and all."

"What do you think Simpson is concealing with such earnestness?"

"The murder of my girl and her girl friend."

"Perhaps that. But what could be his motive for killing them?"

"Having got Simpson's background, I reckon that what's behind them girls getting lost is pretty big. Simpson's a natural killer. He's got the eyes of a killer and the hands of one too. Pa showed me how to pick 'em, men who are just naturally dangerous."

"He can play the organ," Bony said.

"He sure can play the organ."

"How do you react to the idea of counterfeiting?"

"Not big enough. I'm not much interested in the cause of my girl and her friend being done away with. I'm interested mostly in who killed them. That's why I've concentrated on Simpson and around his saloon. The cause, in my opinion, requires a mighty good barbed-wire fence to keep it in and keep them out who might be wanting to uncover it."

"Oh!"

"As I said, I'm not concerned with causes, but only with effects. What I aim to do is to locate the effects. I've located one, but it don't rile me as much as I'm gonna be when I find what's happened to my girl. When she and her pal were first missed, Simpson headed the search for them. I guess the fella that was yardman at the time saw something or added something to something else. His name was O'Brien. He was a little old man with white hair, and he never wore socks. Never wore boots, either, 'cause of his bunions. Ferris told me all about him. A fortnight after the girls disappeared, and when Ferris and her mother were away, O'Brien left. He's an effect. He's buried right under where you're sitting."

CHAPTER XVII

"YOU EVER BEEN IN LOVE?"

BONY stared at the lounging American for three seconds before his gaze fell and his right hand conveyed the cigarette to his lips. For ten seconds Shannon noted that the hand trembled.

One of Bony's burdens, and not the least, was fear of the dead, fear which, during his career of crime investigation, had often leaped from the subconscious to gibber at him, reminding him of the ancient race from which he would never wholly escape.

The American was unaware that it was grossly unfair to spring the information on Bony at this particular time and place, but the whites of the eyes and the trembling hand gave him an inkling of the devil he had loosed. Regret was tinged a little by contempt, and then because there was no tremor in Bony's voice the contempt was banished by admiration.

"How do you know that O'Brien is buried beneath me?"

"Partly through Ferris Simpson, I came to find out about that," Shannon replied. "When Jim Simpson was away I used to talk with Ferris, who's mighty interested in the United States. Knowing there was a yardman employed at the saloon at the time my girl vanished, I asked Ferris what became of him. She told me she wasn't easy about the way O'Brien left when she and her ma were away on a short holiday, and that her pa kept harping about Jim Simpson firing him for being drunk in the spirit store. Ferris said that on returning from that holiday she went to the spirit store and is pretty certain that no one had been in it since she herself was there the day before she went off with her ma."

"What made her certain that no one had entered the store during her absence, d'you know?"

"Yes. There wasn't much stock in the store, and she knew what the stock totalled. There were no broken cases when she went away and none when she returned."

"Then what?" Bony asked, and Shannon's admiration remained, for Bony had not moved an inch from his position over the grave.

"One of my jobs was to take the horse and dray into the forest and bring in firewood. I never had to go a mile away to load the wood, but someone, before I went there to work, had brought the dray right out to this place. You can see where the tracks ended, where the dray was stopped and then taken back. So I mooched around some. I said to myself: 'If I had a body on that dray, where would I plant it?'

"I did a lot of arguing with myself, and I did a lot of trailing around, mostly when the moon gave good light because I could never be sure about Simpson. I came in here one afternoon and seen where a dog had done some scratching and given up. And I went back, not feeling at all good about it.

"You see, if there was a body buried here I couldn't know whether it was that old yardman or my girl. Naturally, I didn't want to do any digging if it was my girl, but I—I had to find out."

Bony shivered. Sometimes imagination is less a gift than a curse. The soft, drawling voice went on:

"I couldn't go on not knowing which of 'em was buried here, if one was. Simpson didn't go off anywhere to give me my chance to find out, and so I came here late one night—and I forgot to bring a spade. You ever been in love?"

Bony's answer was a slow affirmative nodding.

"Sometimes it hurts, being in love," Shannon said. "It sort of numbs a guy's brain and makes him do funny things. It was a funny thing for me to do, to come here that night without a spade, and when I came here I knew that I'd never have guts enough again to come to do what I had to do.

"I set the torch on the boulder over there behind you. I had to shift a deal of sand with my hands and then lift up several stone slabs. I wasn't thinking of much else but what I'd do to someone with my knives if I—if it was my sweetheart. I kept thinking mostly of how a Chinaman ranch cook showed me to use knives without killing.

"Anyway, when I'd gone down two feet I came to hair. The hair came away in my hand, and I had to get up and take it to the torch, and I wasn't feeling too bright, not even when I saw that the hair was white and not light brown with a golden sheen in it like my girl's hair. Still, I wasn't sure, not knowing what being planted would do to hair, and so I went on digging and came to clothes, and the clothes were so perished that still I couldn't be sure which one of 'em it was. It was the shoes that proved it. The canvas was rotten, but the rubber soles were sound enough. O'Brien always wore canvas shoes."

The American used the glowing end of a stick to gain flame for his cigarette, and the vastly grotesque shadow flickered upon the granite ceiling and upon the bulging walls. For a little while he was silent.

"Yes, I guess it hurts sometimes, being in love, I was never in love before I met Mavis Sanky. She was a fine kid. Pa told me to keep smiling till I found out for sure. Well, I been doing my best, and I'm going on that way until I'm sure, sure that she was killed and didn't just perish in this goddamn country. So I replanted old Ted O'Brien exactly as he had been, and I went out backwards and smothered out all the evidence and afterwards sneaked in here now and then to see if the murderer had paid a visit."

"When did you find the body here?" Bony asked.

"It was about a fortnight before you arrived at the saloon. I watched you mooching around the place. How did you know I was watching you?"

"No man walks in this country without leaving his tracks."

"Tracks, eh! I didn't think—— I thought tracks were only on sandy or dusty——"

"It's a gift. The gift of tracking others is a shade less than the gift of leaving no tracks for others to follow. I thought, on seeing you had been observing me, that you were in Simpson's pay. My apology. The old man told me of O'Brien being discharged for being drunk in the spirit store, and I noted the significance of those cart tracks. Why do you think Simpson killed O'Brien?"

"I don't know, unless O'Brien knew he had killed my girl and her pal."

"What happened to cause you to leave the hotel at such speed?"

"So's I wouldn't be caught up with and have something framed to put me in jail. You get a chance to go into the room where Simpson's organ is? No? I did. I unlocked the door with a bit of wire one night when Simpson and his sister were

116

away at Dunkeld. I don't know anything about organs, but I bet that one cost a few thousand bucks. The room's always kept locked and, according to Ferris, no one's ever allowed to go in excepting Simpson's pals. There's only one thing funny about that room, and that's the telephone set on a perch at the side of the organ. There's a fixture to it so's the organist can wear it like radio head-phones and do his talking while he plays the organ to stop anyone hearing him using the telephone.

"Well, when Simpson told me I'd have to quit the next morning it was when we were finishing up dinner. After dinner Simpson went in to play the organ, and I had a hunch that he might be up to tricks with his pals over at Baden Park. Just what, I didn't make out, but I wasn't going to risk being stopped from looking for Mavis. Besides which, Simpson might have guessed I knew about this planting.

"So I decided to quit right then. I packed my gear and took it to the garage. Ferris saw me and wanted to know things. I told her about getting the push-off, and she said I was a wise guy to get going. We talked some more as we cleaned up after dinner, Simpson continuing to play on his organ. I said nothing about finding O'Brien and she said nothing about her brother. It wasn't what she actually said at any time which counted, it was the way she said it and the look in her eye when she said it. I never told her about Mavis and why I'd come back to Australia.

"Anyway, it was dark when I finished up, and as I went to the garage to load the gear on the bike I saw the lights of a car coming over the range from Baden Park. I pushed the bike out of the garage, and there was Simpson waiting for me, wanting to know if I was going for a spin. I told him I was going for good, and he said O.K. and I'd better go in with him for my money.

"He delayed somewhat, telling me I needn't leave till the morning, and when he did pay me the ranch car arrived and three of the boys came in for a drink. They wanted me to stay and drink with 'em, but I walked out on 'em and left. Didn't ride fast, but I did want to get clear."

"Do you know that you were followed as far as the road junction?" Bony asked.

"No. Was I?"

Bony related what he had seen and then asked another question:

"Where did you go that night?"

"To Dunkeld. Stayed at the hotel, and the next morning I bought a quart-pot and stores. Hung around that day and later left to come back to where I hid the bike in the scrub and set out on the war-path."

"You don't think it probable that Simpson might have telephoned to someone in Dunkeld to watch you and report what you did?"

"No. Do you?"

"Yes."

Shannon chuckled and Bony was startled.

"Going to be a good war," he drawled. "Wish Pa was here. Pity you're a cop. You thinking of interfering?"

"Perhaps."

"That's off the target." The American pondered, then said unsmilingly: "You're a good guy, but you don't know how to stick a fella up properly. A character minds less being drilled through the heart than being shot in the stomach. Always keep your gun pointed at a man's stomach. It sort of intimidates. If you ever come to thinking of arresting me, you hedge around the idea."

In his turn Bony chuckled, and Shannon grinned and stood up.

"I'm having an hour or two of shut-eye," he announced. "Oh! What about this cottontail?"

"How long have you had it?" asked Bony.

"How long! Shot him this morning."

"Better bury it. The flies will have got to it."

The American picked up the carcass, turned it to the fire glow.

"You're right, and I'm sick of Simpson's chickens."

"Simpson's chickens?"

"Yep. Visited his hen-houses coupla nights. Pa showed me how to wring a chicken so's he don't squawk. Must get me another, I suppose."

"It might mean the pitcher going too often to the well."

"I know that one. Pa usta say: 'Never mind the pitcher, it's the water that counts.'"

Bony added the last of the wood to give light and, picking

up his swag, carried it to the passage. Shannon joined him there and they made up their bunks together.

"Don't much fancy camping too close to Ted O'Brien," Shannon said casually. "Don't fancy that place anyhow, after looking him over. I'd like to know for sure just why he was bumped off."

"We will," Bony said.

"You think so?"

"Yes. I always investigate a murder to the very end."

"Always get your man!"

"Always."

"You aim to copy the Canadian Mounties, eh?"

"Not copy them, Shannon. I have always set the example which they try to copy. I shall establish who killed O'Brien and why, and who killed your sweetheart and her friend—if they were killed. You must realise that if you conduct a private war, as you name your proposed activities, and I discover you have killed someone, I shall be obliged to arrest you or have you arrested."

"I'll have to go careful, won't I?"

There was mockery in Shannon's voice and extraordinary good humour.

"Very careful," and only with an effort did Bony keep his voice stern. "In view of your great personal interest, with the addition of other circumstances favourable to you, the best course to follow would be for me to call upon you, in the King's name, to assist me in apprehending certain suspected persons—if in the plural. Not being unintelligent, you will appreciate how far I am willing to go when I add that if, during the process of apprehension, your pistol should be discharged with fatal effect, the results to yourself will be much less unpleasant."

"What a guy!" murmured the American. "One hundred words!"

"Under those circumstances you will not use your pistol unless and until you receive my permission."

"Sounds a bit tough to me. What about my throat-cutters?"

"They, too, are considered to be lethal weapons."

"You're telling me." Shannon stretched and bumped a hole in the sand to take his hip. "I like freedom, and you sound too army-ish. What did we fight for? Search me, but the idea at the time was freedom. I've lots to think about when considering your proposition. There's Pa, for one. He considers my girl one of the family. I gotta consider Pa's principles and the family. I'm leaving the causes to you. You can do what you like with the causes behind the killing of my girl and her pal—assuming they were killed, which I am assuming. Them that killed my girl are mine to do to just what I like."

Bony stretched. A freedom for which his feet ached was freedom from boots, but boots are necessary adjuncts in the bush. He said with a bite in his voice:

"What a guy. I ought to arrest you and conduct you to the lock-up at Dunkeld and charge you with being a walking arsenal. I have listened to your threats to disturb the peace and, too, interfere with a police officer in the execution of his duty. Candidly, I'd like you to work with me, but in accordance with my over-all instructions. Mine is the responsibility to the constituted authority."

Shannon said sleepily:

"I'll think it over, buddy. You're a good guy, even though you are a cop. What's your real name?"

"You may call me Bony."

"Bony what?"

"Just Bony."

"Bony it is. We'll rub along O.K. Pleasure to work with a guy who sets a good example to the Canadian Mounties."

Silence for thirty seconds, and then the low and regular snoring of an American "character", the like of whom Bony had never met. The red embers of the fire stained the walls of Edward O'Brien's vault with the colour of the blood which doubtless seeped from him. In the short passage between the chamber of death and that leading to the good clean air, Bony and his companion lay in darkness.

Bony was exceedingly tired. His body ached. Again and again he almost fell asleep, only to flash back into keen wakefulness as the items of information given by Shannon marshalled themselves for re-examination.

When the American stirred and ceased to snore the silence worried the wakeful man, the silence and that instinctive fear of the dead lying within a dozen feet of him. Once repose was beaten off by the thought that Shannon could have mastered him physically on several occasions, and then he came wide awake to find himself compelled to look at the picture of Shannon scooping with his hands and a stick in the sand.

Because he could not see the stars, he could not see the time. The red walls and the roof of the rock chamber imperceptibly faded into the colour of a pall, leaving the darkness to press heavily on him. Twice he sat up and blindly rolled a cigarette, and with the flame of the matches assured himself that Shannon was still there. He decided the dawn must be at hand and was thinking of going out to see if his snares had trapped a rabbit, when he heard an exterior noise which froze his body.

The silence crowded back upon him, and he raised himself to lean upon an elbow. Then he heard it again, the distant creaking of dray wheels. He reached for Shannon, and the American said:

"Bit early to come for a load of firewood."

CHAPTER XVIII

FEAR OF THE DEAD

SHANNON must have glanced at his wrist-watch, for he said:
"Ten past four. Wonder what's on the ice."

"Pack your kit," Bony commanded. "We may have to move
in a hurry." The American uttered a "But——" and was
faintly surprised by the brittleness of Bony's voice, a note
absent even when he was bailed up at pistol-point. "Don't
talk. Pack."

In the pitch blackness they worked on their gear to the
accompaniment of the increasing noise of the dray. They
heard the hotel licensee curse the horse.

"Simpson!" Shannon said with soft sibilance.

"Your quart-pot," snapped Bony, pushing the utensil
against him. "A few yards along the passage, on your right,
there's a space between the rocks. Take the swags and leave
them there. Then go to the entrance and watch Simpson."

Shannon departed, dragging the swags with him, impressed
by Bony's abruptly assumed authority. Without light Bony
entered the chamber on his hands and knees and made his way
to the site of the now cold fire. Feeling for it with his hands
and finding it, he scooped a hole in the sand, dragged into the
hole the ashes and the semi-burned wood, then, covering the
hole, threw handfuls of sand upon the site.

The necessity for speed blunted the horror Shannon had
created with words and, still on hands and knees, he worked
smoothing out the tracks on the sandy floor and giving a final
touch by flicking a towel over the surface. Having done all
possible within the chamber and withdrawing from it legs
first, he worked back along the short passage to its junction
with the main passage, the floor of which was covered with
granite chips. There he paused swiftly to survey mentally
what he had done that nothing should be left undone to betray
Shannon and himself.

He joined the American, who was standing just inside the

"front entrance". Simpson had made a fire by the creek, and the light enabled them to see him bring from the creek a kerosene tin filled with water. The horse was still harnessed to the dray near-by. Tiny electrical impulses flashed up and down at the back of Bony's neck as Simpson set the tin of water against the fire and then took from the dray an enamel basin, a towel, and a cake of soap.

"Shall I start in on him?" whispered Shannon.

"Certainly not. What did you do when you came out after filling in the grave?"

"Washed my——" Breath hissed between the American's teeth. "You reckon he's come to transplant the body?"

"It's probable. Do nothing to stop him. If he comes this way I'll go in ahead of him. You lie low—where you are. Look!"

Simpson lifted from the dray a hurricane lamp and a shovel and came towards the mountain of rocks. The American melted into the void between two boulders, and Bony backed silently down the passage and waited at the first bend. He saw Simpson appear at the entrance, silhouetted by his fire, and there the licensee dropped the shovel and lit the lamp. He was wearing old and tattered slacks, a grey flannel under-vest, and a pair of old shoes. His hair was roughed and his cold grey eyes were small.

The hand which had held the match to the lamp was shaking, and the lamp itself trembled in the other. He came two paces inside and then uttered an expletive and set the lamp down so violently it was almost extinguished. He went out again and Bony waited. On returning, he was carrying a partly filled sack.

The sack, in addition to the shovel and the lamp, was quite a load to manœuvre through the passage, and as the licensee progressed, Bony went backwards before him, never once moving a betraying stone until, arriving at the space where Shannon had placed the swags, he slewed into it and laid himself flat. Simpson passed him on his way to the chamber, and instantly Bony rose and stole after him, gambling on the man's nervous tension preventing him from seeing the necessarily rough efforts to clean the sandy floor.

It was a sure thing that the man would not spend time on anything save the main objective, and with all haste governed by natural caution, Bony reached the short passage to the chamber, edged his face round a corner of granite, and became one with the rock.

The lamp was set on a low ledge, and the shovel was lying on the place where Bony had sat with his back against his swag. Against the creviced roof and the broken walls a monstrous shadow writhed like something on a gridiron over a Dante's hell. From the sack Simpson was withdrawing a roll of light canvas, and this he spread upon the ground between the grave and the entrance. Also from the sack he drew a waterproof sheet, which he arranged on the canvas, and a quantity of heavy twine rolled round a short length of board.

Bony had never before seen a man's face so tortured. Simpson stood with his back to the site of Bony's fire, his eyes wide and brilliant as they surveyed the preparations. He was not quite satisfied with the waterproof sheet upon the canvas, and his eyes moved rapidly to find something with which to overcome a difficulty. Then, when he lifted a heavy stone and dropped it upon one corner of the square of canvas and sheet, and another stone on the second corner nearer the scene of the intended operation, Bony knew the difficulty and the necessity to overcome it.

One who appreciates music and can play it as Simpson could is the antithesis of the exhumator. His breathing was laboured, and as though he realised that this could not go on and had foreseen it, he managed to take from a pocket a flask of spirits, draw the cork with his teeth, and swallow the entire contents as one might swallow water.

Then the work began.

Without conscious volition Bony's feet turned away from the horror. His body became as iron to the magnet of the pure night without, so that with his hands he was obliged, without being conscious of it, to grasp projections of the rocky corner that he might continue to watch. A thousand demons came to tug him away. The electrical impulses which had been playing up and down his neck became needles of ice lodged into the base of his skull. Instincts became sentient beings that warred about him and for him. The fear of the dead was like an octopus wrapping its tentacles about his brain, compressing it into a pin-head of matter in the centre of a vast and otherwise empty skull. And somewhere beyond the void a million voices sped to him along the aisles of Time, screaming to him to run.

The mission baby who grew up to the boy who played and adventured with the aborigines, who went away to high school in the city, who spent every vacation with the aborigines to study the great Book of the Bush, who passed into the university and out again with a brilliant record, who went bush for three years to perfect himself for his intended profession, had become a man who commanded the ice to melt and the demons to flee and the voices to be hushed, commanded and was not obeyed.

Into the heat and the cold, the turmoil and the terror, came the voice of Detective-Inspector Napoleon Bonaparte, saying stiltedly:

"I employ my talents with nothing short of major crimes. I have never failed to finalise a case. A murder has been committed and there, before my eyes, this murder and this murderer are the effects of a cause. To arrest this murderer now is unlikely to establish the cause, the motive for the crime, the pattern into which it fits—must fit. Why Simpson murdered O'Brien is of less import than why Simpson is now digging up his victim. Murder often begets murder, and this is the one begotten."

"Run!" screamed the million voices. "Don't look! Turn your head! Run, or you'll see the picture you'll never forget."

"Must stay! Watch! Wait!" commanded Inspector Bonaparte. "Be still! You are a man. Simpson is a man no longer. Look at him!"

Simpson had dug out the sand and had removed the stones. Like a monstrous insect, he was dragging his victim towards the spread sheets. Backwards he went, crouched, his two arms stretched taut, as though he must keep the horror he dragged as far from him as possible. He had dragged it to within a yard of the nearer edge of the sheets when it parted about the middle, and all movement abruptly ceased, save the movement of the living man's eyes alternately directing their gaze from that part of the thing still clutched in his hands and that part which had been left behind.

Simpson backed on to the spread sheets and dragged the thing over their edges, the heavy stones he had placed keeping those edges to the ground. Then he returned for the remainder and dragged that upon the sheet, slowly, as though knowing that haste would part it also.

What happened now was akin to the screened film abruptly rushed into abnormal speed. Simpson flung himself down and whipped one edge of the waterproof sheet over the dreadful remains, rolled and rolled, flung inward the sides, and rolled again. He leaped to the far side, his breathing hissing like escaping steam, his body doubled upon itself so that his arms and legs were in proportion, like those of a spider. Snatching up the hem of the under sheet, he proceeded to roll the bundle in it, tucking in the ends. He leaped upon the twine, snatched it from the ground where he had so carefully placed it, and bound and bound it about the bundle.

The knots were tied, and he straightened up, his chest heaving, his lungs fighting for air, his mind struggling to maintain sanity, to return from the pit of obscenity. Once he looked at his hands, and his stomach sharply deflated, like that of a dog vomiting. Then, springing upon the spade, he worked like a man beneath the flailing whips of the Gestapo.

Having filled in the vacant grave, he smoothed the surface. The spade he pushed into an opening between the wall rocks. The bag he pushed inward after the spade. The lamp he picked up and looped the handle from the elbow of his left arm. He stooped and picked up the bundle.

Bony retreated, not unlike a sleep-walker, his conscious mind seemingly disenthroned. His body conducted his brain along the passage, took it into the space where were the swags, laid itself down. Then nausea triumphed, and the bonds were broken and the ice needles melted.

He saw Simpson pass with the lamp and his burden, fought with nausea, smothered his face in the towel he had used to smooth away the tracks. Shannon's heavy pack was beside him and he moved so that it was beneath his stomach, and an aid to prevent the retching and the noise of it, till Simpson was clear of the little mountain of rocks.

Presently he felt better. The pack remained a comfort and he lay still whilst the turmoil subsided. A waft of cool air fanned his wet face and neck. The dead had departed, gone on the back of the living, and with it passed fear of the dead. The dawn wind was blowing through the passage, coming down through all the crevices, sweeping away the smell of the dead.

Lurching to his feet, Bony leaned against a rock wall and was forced to wait whilst strength mounted within him. To him was the tribute that as he made his way to the entrance not once did a stone betray his passing.

Shannon was watching from the entrance. He said nothing, and Bony leaned against a rock and was glad to do so. Simpson's fire was leaping high. The horse and dray were still close by. There was nothing of Simpson. The bundle was not in view, nor was the lamp. In the air was the stink of burning cloth.

"Gone to the creek," Shannon said softly. "He put what he brought out into the dray. Then he stripped and tossed his clothes and shoes into the fire. Then he picked up the soap and the can of hot water and went over to the creek. Quite a character."

Bony made no comment and Shannon asked:

"Did he dig it up?"

"Yes," Bony managed to say, and found relief in the power to speak.

"Must be going to plant it some place else," surmised the American. "I'd like to know what happened to make him take on the job. The old guy was comfortable enough where he was. No one would have found him."

"You did," Bony pointed out, and added: "I would have done so."

They observed Simpson coming from the creek into the radius of the firelight. His powerful body glistened with water. They watched him towelling himself. They watched him dress in clothes and shoes contained in another sack and, having dressed, from the sack draw a bottle from which he drank, and a tin of cigarettes, one of which he lit, standing with his back to the blaze whilst he smoked.

"We gonna tail him?" whispered Shannon.

"No need to. We can track the dray."

Simpson was gazing towards them, and for the moment Bony thought he had detected their presence. Then he saw that Simpson was regarding the crest of the range against the sky, seeing the serrated line of black velvet against the heavenly opal of the dawn.

He smoked another cigarette and drank long from the bottle, and by now the youthful day was struggling with the ancient night. Simpson flexed his arms and opened his shoulders, as though from the growing day he took strength and poise into himself. He tossed bottle and towel and basin into the sack, and the sack he carried to the dray.

He led the horse away. Bony and the American continued to stand at the entrance of the desecrated pyramid, listening to the diminishing sound of creaking wheels. A bellbird offered its tinkling chimes to the glory of the day.

"I'm going in for the swags," Bony said. "You make a fire down the creek, away from that fire."

"Do we brew some coffee and eat?" Shannon asked.

"You may eat, certainly," Bony replied. "Strong tea is what I need, as a drowning man needs air."

"Two drops and a half of bourbon is what we both need, Bony, old pal. There's a bottle of brandy in my pack. Did you see Simpson doing his digging?"

"I did. Brandy, did you say? Did you say you had brandy in your pack?"

"A full and unopened bottle."

"I wonder, Shannon, that I can wait. Yes, I watched Simpson. It wasn't nice. I've been very sick."

Shannon nodded. He said:

"Be easy, pal. I'll fetch the packs. You're as tough as hell."

CHAPTER XIX

SIMPSON'S SUPERIOR

"You going to nail Simpson for killing the old guy?" Shannon asked, when he was eating damper bread and a tin of pork and beans and Bony was sipping his third pannikin of tea, laced with brandy.

"No. I must know Simpson's motive for moving the body. It must be a tremendously powerful one and so remarkable that I am unable even to theorise about it. However, Simpson is continuing to make a pattern, and he must be permitted to go on making the pattern until the motive appears in it."

"Show me the pattern, and eat a slice of this damn fine bread to sort of soak up the brandy you're tearing into you."

"The suggestion is sound. Thank you. The pattern, yes. It begins that morning the two girls left the hotel. Simpson made sure that Ferris was with him when the girls left and that subsequently he was observed repairing the garage. He made sure it was on record that he stood by Price's car and talked with him just when he was leaving. He probably murdered O'Brien when his mother and sister were absent on holiday and his old father was incapable of keeping him under observation. He was absent when his city henchmen arrived and insulted the lady artist. He was absent when his henchmen attempted to assault me. We don't, of course, know what his plan was with reference to yourself, but I believe it would have conformed to the general plan of providing himself with an alibi."

"You think he was intending to have me done in?" Shannon asked.

"Don't you?"

"I reckon—by his pals at Baden Park."

"But not, I think, by the owners of Baden Park. In fact, I cannot believe that he telephoned for those men who came over that night—until and unless I have much stronger evidence. Now answer me this: Was anyone present when Simpson told you you would have to leave?"

"Yes, the old man."

"Then he told you that you could stay that night and go in the morning. After that he withdrew to play the organ, having no design upon you, as he had not given himself time to plan an alibi and arrange for you to be dealt with *à la* the detective. He did speak with Baden Park and learned that three of the men were coming over for the evening. They arrived when you were about to leave. He couldn't stop you. With some tale or other that you had gone off with the petty cash, or had insulted Ferris, or something else, he induced them to give chase, to find out which road you had taken from the junction. And on his return he telephoned a pal in Dunkeld to report on what you did, just to be sure you had or had not left the district.

"He was informed that you purchased provisions and a quart-pot and that you came this way on leaving Dunkeld. He recalled that you had done quite a lot of bush walking and that he had seen your tracks in the vicinity where he had buried O'Brien.

"I've no doubt that he did have a plan to do you in, as you say, and he acted a little too hastily in telling you to leave, in the first place, and in the second you declined to accept his invitation to remain until the next day. Those two causes produce a fault in the plan showing that Simpson, in all previous instances, had a perfect alibi."

"H'm!" Shannon grunted, lighting a cigarette. "You reckon he done like Pa usta advise me and the kid brother never to do; get drunk or chase the girls in the old home town, that being bad for respectability?"

"That, I think, circumscribes the idea," Bony said, smiling for the first time that morning. "Old Simpson mentioned to me that there are hard doers, or dangerous men, in this country. Some of them might well be among the stockmen at Baden Park, but it isn't logical to include with them Mr. Carl Benson, the owner of the very valuable Baden Park Station and all its golden fleeces. Our interest must lie in and about the hotel, and in Simpson and his associates, or those of them desperate enough to commit murder."

"Then why that mighty fine fence around Baden Park?" asked the American.

"The fence is a legitimate insurance against the theft of valuable animals and the depredations of wild dogs. The electrically-controlled gate is quite a good idea, because people will leave gates open, no matter how the pastoralist might plead or command with a notice affixed to his gates. Are you sure that, having found the body of O'Brien, you obliterated all the signs?"

"Yes, I am."

"Simpson, remember, was born and reared in this country. He is a bushman, and it is therefore certain that he saw your tracks, plainly indicating that you had often been in this locality, and possibly was so informed of your entry into that mound of rocks. When he discharged you and then wanted you to remain until the next morning, either a plan concerning you went wrong or he's far from sure that you discovered anything of significance. In this particular instance he acted out of character, and that is a point which will require attention.

"We do know that Simpson has removed an illegally-buried body. We can assume that Simpson murdered O'Brien. We are entitled to assume that the murder of O'Brien is a natural corollary of the murder of Detective Price and/or the murder of those two young women. But assumption is as far as we can go. Price *could* have been killed by a criminal whom he recognised. The girls could remain undiscovered for years, if ever found."

"Getting yourself all tied up, aren't you?" Shannon cut in, the corners of his mouth hinting at grim humour.

"No," Bony replied. "I am merely proceeding with caution to avoid the possibility of taking a wrong track and thus wasting time. You are inclined to think that that party of men from Baden Park were sent for by Simpson. We must remember that previously Simpson sent to Melbourne for his thugs to persuade a lady artist and myself to leave the hotel."

"But this time his plug-uglies are in the hands of the cops," countered Shannon.

"Doubtless he could have arranged for others. Anyway, we are not progressing, and there is Simpson to follow and establish what he has done with the body. When your girl set out on the trip through these mountains she was wearing a hair-clip set with red brilliants. Did you know that?"

"Yes. I gave her the ornament."

"I found a red brilliant within a few minutes of finding the piece of stone with the gold in it."

Shannon's blue eyes opened wide for a moment and then contracted.

"Is that so?" he said very slowly.

"I found it where a car had been turned on the area of quartz. It could have been waiting for those girls. During a struggle the trinket could have fallen from the girl's head and been trampled upon. The trinket could have been picked up and the brilliant from it not noticed."

"Have you got the brilliant with you?"

"No. It's in safe hands. I think, Shannon, it would be wise for you to continue searching for traces of those two girls, and I will continue my investigation into the motives and actions of Simpson. If you will do that and promise not to take the law into your own hands, we will progress much better. We will leave our swags here, concealing them with scrub, and we could meet here again late this evening to make camp and compare notes."

"Okey doke. Let's act."

Eventually, the swags were hidden among a nest of rocks at the foot of the range, and when returning to the creek to pick up the tracks of the dray, Bony pointed out the tracks left by the American.

"Pretty hard for an ordinary guy to trail a man through this country," countered Shannon, and not for the first time revealing a stubborn streak.

"Good Australian bushmen are not ordinary guys, Shannon. Australian aborigines are super-extraordinary guys. However, we are fortunate that there are no aborigines in this district— so far as I know. Well, now, I'm going after that dray. We'll act independently. Meet you tonight."

Shannon nodded agreement a trifle too casually to satisfy Bony and at once proceeded to demonstrate his bushcraft by disappearing into the scrub. Bony went forward, keeping roughly parallel with the dray's tracks, for him broken bush and scrub being a clear guide.

It was quickly evident that Simpson had not led the horse

towards the hotel, but had skirted the foot of the range, reaching the elbow of the side track where it left the vineyard, and then, on that track, had passed through the white gates he had left open. Keeping wide of the track, Bony found the horse and dray standing on a small cleared space, and the licensee sitting with his back against a stack of some six tons of cut firewood.

Bony concealed himself in a patch of low bush at the edge of the clearing, and he, too, made himself comfortable, envying Simpson his opportunity to smoke. He had seen and heard nothing of Shannon.

The stack of wood was significant and confronted Bony with a problem. Should he prevent the destruction by fire of the yardman's remains? Where lay his duty? If the body was destroyed by all that wood, what then? Fire does not completely destroy a human body. The calcined bones remain among the ashes, and teeth, natural or artificial, and such items as metal buttons and boot nails.

Because he felt that O'Brien's murder was the outcome of others, because he felt that through Simpson and his crime he would penetrate the mystery covering the fate of the two girls, he decided again to lie low, like Br'er Rabbit.

A full hour passed, and he was fighting off sleep and yawning for a cigarette, when he heard the sound of horse's hooves coming down the road from Baden Park. Simpson did not budge, although he must have heard the approaching horseman. He did not rise until the horseman reined off the road and dismounted beside the dray.

The rider was tall and lean and slightly grizzled. Bony had seen him twice before, seated with a woman in a magnificent Rolls-Royce.

CHAPTER XX

THE MAN FROM BADEN PARK

THERE was no friendliness in the greeting. Simpson stood before the horseman with a scowl on his face. The horseman regarded Simpson with a steady glare in agate-hard blue eyes, and there was a tautness in his body foreign to the Australian pastoralist whose garb he wore. His voice was resonant.

"You brought the body?"

"Yes. It's in the dray. I rolled it in canvas."

"Place it on the heap of wood and unroll it that I may inspect it."

"Oh, I brought it all right," Simpson snapped, rebellion in his eyes.

"That I may inspect it," repeated the horseman.

Simpson shrugged, and from the dray drew the corded bundle on to a shoulder and carried it to the woodstack. The stack was four feet high, and he heaved the bundle upon it, sprang to the top of the stack, and, cutting the cords, obeyed the order. There was none of the horror in his eyes and on his face Bony had seen in that dark hour before the dawn. There was now rebellion and anger that his word had been doubted. The sun was shining. The birds were awake and excited. And there was a living man beside him, the horseman having agilely mounted the woodstack.

"Satisfied?" Simpson flung over his shoulder.

No alteration occurred on the face of the horseman. He replied:

"Proceed with the burning."

He jumped to earth and Simpson followed. The horseman strode stiffly to his horse and led it farther from the dray and nearer to Bony. From the dray Simpson took a four-gallon tin and proceeded to pour the contents on the woodstack along that side facing the wind. With a match he fired a piece of brushwood, and this he tossed against the petrol-drenched wood. Then, placing the empty drum into the dray, he led the horse a little way down the road.

The wood had been cut perhaps two years and was over-cured for cooking purposes. After the first emission of black smoke it sent up tenuous blue smoke, which the wind carried to the range and dispersed against the granite face.

The horseman relaxed, standing on the road with the bridle rein looped over his forearm and watching the mounting fire. He must have seen Simpson approaching from the parked horse and dray, for without speaking he produced a cigarette-case and proffered it. The licensee accepted a cigarette from the gold case, which sparkled with a bluish light of diamonds. Neither spoke as they watched the woodstack burning.

The pyre presently became a great, slowly-subsiding mass of coals. There was no smoke, only the hot air rising in a long slant. The object of bringing the body all this distance to burn was plain. The wood of the stack was dust-dry and no longer contained gas, and thus gave off a minimum of smoke, it being the end of summer, when smoke is likely to bring a spotting aeroplane.

Carl Benson broke the long silence, and from his voice had gone the brittleness.

"The work is well done, Jim. An unpleasant episode is almost finished. You must attend to the final details tomorrow morning."

"You going to trust me to do it, or are you coming along to watch me?" Simpson almost snarled.

It did seem that Carl Benson was impervious to the other's mood, for neither his face nor his voice changed by a fraction.

"I am not sorry that I spoke coldly," he said. "You must not resent my orders or my displeasure, because our trust is too great to permit our reactions to situations to affect it. Yours was the mistake, mine and yours the task of rectifying it."

"All right, Carl. I'm sorry I was huffy. It was a filthy job and, I now see, necessary. You can depend on me to recover the bones in the morning and put them through a prospector's dolly-pot and toss away the dust."

"Of course, it was a horrible business, Jim, but there was nothing else for it. I was angry because you did not report at the time the removal of that old fool, and for dealing with the corpse in the way you did and thus creating danger to the consummation of The Plan."

"The chance of finding the body where I planted it was a thousand to one."

"Agreed, Jim. But the one chance in the thousand could not be accepted in view of the Trust laid upon us. And, further, I am not pleased by the manner in which you got rid of that American. You acted hastily and without proper thought, when you should have accepted my guidance. However, have you seen or heard anything of him?"

"No, not after Amos reported that he had left Dunkeld and taken the road out this way. It's likely that he went to Hall's Gap."

"We cannot be sure of that," Benson said. "We have no one there now to report, since Lockyer left. And thus we have to proceed with extreme caution until the culmination of The Plan on the twenty-eighth. Come over tonight and play for us. The company will help the music to get this business out of your system."

"But I will be with you tomorrow night," Simpson objected half-heartedly.

"No matter. Come tonight too. There are one or two items I would like to arrange before tomorrow night."

"All right! Thanks, I will. I'll be in the mood for Wagner."

Benson flicked the reins over the horse's head. He held out his left hand and Simpson accepted it.

"We have both made one very bad mistake," he said. "Yours was the old yardman, mine was in acquiescing to Cora's demands. Your mistake will have been completely eliminated tomorrow morning, when you dispose of the residue of that fire. My mistake still waits to be rectified. We will discuss the matter this evening."

Mounting, Carl Benson nodded down at Simpson, and Simpson raised his right hand in partial salute, nodded in return, and strode away to the dray. The dust of the road rose in little puff-balls behind the departing horseman.

Simpson returned to the fire, which he circled slowly and with evident satisfaction. There was no need to push inward unburned ends of wood, for the stack had burned evenly and now was a low mound of white ash and overlying red coals. By nightfall it might be sufficiently cold to prospect for items similar to those which in the past had brought men to the gallows. Of a certainty the harvesting could be done on the morrow.

Bony wondered where, precisely, Shannon was at that moment. Although from concealment anywhere near the clearing he could have seen and recognised the horseman, he could not have overheard the conversation. That was just as well, for the American could not be permitted to enter upon a private war before all the threads of this tangled skein were in his, Bony's, hands.

The implications of the recent meeting in conjunction with the pyre were .truly tremendous. That Simpson, a hotel-keeper, should murder his yardman was astonishing enough, but that the owner of Baden Park Station and the famous Grampian strain of sheep should be associated with murder caused Bony to compel himself to relax in order to accept and assess it. The man had spoken of two mistakes as one speaking of betting mistakes, and one of the mistakes was not being informed of a murder that he could have guided the murderer in disposing of the body. He had mentioned a trust which was his and Simpson's, responsibility to which overshadowed a murder, and which was so great that a murderer was forced to dig up his victim in the night and transport the remains to destroy them with fire.

What Carl Benson's one mistake could have been in surrendering to some demand made by his sister was beyond the power of Bony's imagination.

There were those other men, the riders who had met at the gate to return in company to the homestead. The picture of the younger man talking to Simpson in his car flooded Bony's mind. Simpson had been angry. He had complained of something to the rider, who had nodded in sympathy and who, as the car moved away, had called: "I don't envy you your job."

The job! Had Simpson gone that afternoon to Baden Park to confess his mistake? Had Benson then ordered him to disinter the body and transport it to the woodstack for destruction? If so, if that was the complaint made by Simpson to the rider, then the rider was aware of the trust which so affected both Benson and Simpson. And, likely enough, the other fellow also was aware of it, and still others in Benson's employ.

It was big, very big. If those two girls were killed because they learned something of this trust, if that woman artist was insulted in order to persuade her to leave or give the excuse for ordering her to leave, and himself assaulted to be rid of him, if Price had been killed because he had discovered something of vital importance, then anyone discovered investigating too closely would meet ruthless treatment, not at the hands of one man, Simpson, but at the hands of Benson and perhaps a dozen of his riders.

He felt that Shannon was capable of looking after himself, although not sufficiently a bushman to conceal his tracks from the average bushman. He himself would be able to outwit a dozen riders, given just ordinary luck, but assuming that during a moment of ill luck he was discovered and either captured or killed, to whom would pass the information he had gathered? Ought he not to leave a record of what he had discovered with Groves, the policeman at Dunkeld, to circumvent the possibility that he fail?

No horse shied away from a fluttering rag as violently as Bonaparte shied away from this word "fail". To fail meant damnation, sure and complete. Failure would dethrone Pride, when nothing would be left him.

Pride drove him on to withstand the idea of reporting his progress to the police. Pride lured him onward to battle alone, promising great rewards, blinding him to the several results to others should he fail.

He saw Simpson walk away to the horse and dray and, glancing at the sun, noted the time. He was suddenly conscious that he was both hungry and in need of a cigarette, and it was when Simpson began to lead the horse down the road towards the gate that he himself began the manufacture of a cigarette.

The dray wheels creaked, and Bony knew that if he lived for a hundred years he would feel his blood chill by a similar noise. He smoked and watched the man and dray pass through the gateway, saw Simpson lock the gates and pocket the key. He heard the creaking wheels for some time after man and dray had disappeared.

For another hour he remained in concealment, watching the birds to tell if Shannon were close. And then, as cautiously as he had hitherto moved through the bush, he made his way back to the nest of rocks where the swags had been left.

Shannon's swag was gone. His own was there, and against it was tilted the partly filled bottle of brandy.

CHAPTER XXI

THE FRIGHTENED MAN

BONY slept for six hours, despite the stealthy March flies and a few inquisitive ants, waking when the sun was setting in a hot sky and the birds by the whispering creek were expressing satisfaction with their day. Having made a smokeless fire and placed thereon his billy for a brew of tea, he shaved and then stripped and bathed in the creek, returning to his cooking fire refreshed physically and mentally and tempted to whistle to express his satisfaction with his day.

Shannon loomed as prominently in his mind as Carl Benson. His liking for the American was begotten in the main by the sentimental streak in his make-up, played upon by the romance of a young ex-soldier setting out alone across the world to prove what had happened to his sweetheart. Beyond the sentimentality of that, Bony, the police officer, could not approve of "private wars" and civilian citizens "mooching" around, when loaded heavily with pistols and throwing knives. The knives displayed in the hotel and the pistol with its ungainly silencer attachment more recently displayed caused him to be thankful that Shannon was not on the warpath against him.

That Shannon had not been sufficiently close to overhear the conversation between Simpson and Carl Benson, if, indeed, he had actually witnessed the burning of the body, was cause for satisfaction. Like all official investigators of crime, Bony felt aversion to amateur detectives.

A greater problem than Shannon, however, was O'Brien's skeleton buried in the cooling ashes of Simpson's fire. On the morrow Simpson would remove the remains and pound them to dust in a prospector's dolly-pot, a utensil shaped like a gun shell, in which stone is reduced to dust and then washed to ascertain its gold content. Once the licensee had done that with the old man's bones, evidence of the crime would be merely circumstantial, resting on the word of two witnesses, plus the possible salvage of clothes buttons and the metal eyelets from the victim's canvas shoes.

The result of moving the dead man's remains from the ashes was obvious. Simpson would report the removal to Carl Benson. They would know that the crime had been discovered, and whatever it was which motivated them would be destroyed, rehidden, or otherwise placed far from them. Bony decided that to remove the remains from the ashes would be a mistake, but just how serious he could not estimate. On the other hand, to leave them for Simpson to destroy might also be a mistake subsequently to be regretted. The issue was decided by the Emperor Napoleon Bonaparte's advice: "When in doubt, do nothing."

That Simpson had murdered the old yardman without the knowledge of Carl Benson, that Benson was an accessory after the fact, and that Simpson was so controlled by Benson as to obey that order to disinter the body and burn it had been made perfectly clear during their meeting at the pyre. And, finally, what actuated a man like Carl Benson to be implicated in murder must be unique in motives. The Carl Bensons of this world and time do not become accessories after the fact—of murder—unless governed by an extremely powerful motive.

It was when rolling his swag that sight of the brandy decided Bony to call on old Simpson and endeavour to extract from him further information concerning the owner of Baden Park, and when he seated himself with his back against that tree which Shannon had employed for a knife-throwing target, the world was dark beneath a sky still containing a little light.

It was twenty minutes after eight when Simpson passed in his car on the way to spend the evening at Baden Park, and it was nine o'clock when Bony circled the hotel, mystified because it was entirely empty of illumination.

As the Buick had passed him he had observed Simpson at the wheel, light from the instrument panel bringing his face into sharp relief. He had not seen passengers, but Mrs. Simpson and Ferris could have been in the rear seat. That they had retired to bed and were asleep thus early could not be assumed.

Quite without sound Bony mounted the front veranda steps, and he was proceeding soundlessly along the veranda when the cockatoo said sleepily, but distinctly:

"Get to hell outa here!"

On reaching the corner, Bony waited, listening, one hand resting against the roof support. He remained there for five minutes, hearing not a sound to indicate movement within the house, the night itself containing only the croaking of frogs along the creek.

Soundlessly, he left the veranda corner and moved to the open french window of old Simpson's bedroom. On the threshold he halted, listening and hearing nothing within, not even the old man's breathing. He took one step into the room. He raised his right foot to take the second step when he was stopped by a thin scream of terror, which faded into a struggle for articulation.

"No—not now, Jim! Not now, Jim! Leave your old father be. I done nothing wrong, son. I said nothing, Jim, not a word, not even a whisper. Don't stand there like that. I can see you, Jim, standing against the windows. I been asleep, Jim. I been——"

The voice from the bed was cut off, and Bony knew that air was being taken into the old lungs to be again expelled in the scream. In that moment of silence he said as he strode to the foot of the bed:

"Stop it! It's John Parkes. It's all right. Jim's gone to Baden Park."

The old man began to sob, and his sobbing was almost as bad as his screaming. Bony returned to the french windows, to stand there listening for sounds of human movement without and beyond the bedroom door. When the sobbing stopped, the silence was a weight.

On returning to the bed, Bony asked the whereabouts of the invalid's wife and daughter, and when the old man replied terror haunted his quavering voice.

"They're away," he said tremulously. "They went off yestiddy. Jim sent 'em to Melbun for a week. Hey! You sure you're John Parkes? You—you're not Jim, are you? Go on, talk. Let me hear your voice."

"No one else in the house bar you?" Bony asked, as he passed to the side of the bed and sat down. He felt a groping hand touch his arm, slide down to the wrist, become clamped about his hand. The old man sighed with relief, attempted to speak, failed, tried again, and mastered his terror.

"It's John Parkes, all right," he said. "What you doing here?"

"Anyone else in the house?"

"No. Did you bring a drink?"

"Thought you might like one. Why aren't you asleep?"

"Sleep! I daren't sleep. Gimme a drink—quick. Can't you tell I'm all in, lyin' here waitin'—waitin'—waitin' for——"

"Waitin' for what?" prompted Bony.

"Oh, nuthin' much. Me imagination's bad tonight. You know, bein' all alone in this big house. Gimme a steadier, John Parkes, and tell me what you been doin' and all."

Bony felt about the bedside table, found a tumbler with a little water in it, added brandy to the water, and passed the glass to the eager hand. Pity stirred within him when he heard the ecstasy which followed.

"Didn't you take your sleeping-tablets tonight?" he asked, and the old man tittered and was silent for a space. When he spoke the fear was back in his voice.

"Jim sent the women away. Musta made up his mind sort of sudden. Took 'em to Stawell early yestiddy afternoon. I got to thinking about that time they went away when Ted O'Brien was found drunk in the spirit store. This time there wasn't no Ted O'Brien. There wasn't no Glen Shannon, either. There was no one. Only me."

"Well, he could look after you," Bony observed. "Why worry?"

"Yes. Jim can always look after me. Too right. Jim can look after me. Cooked me a good dinner tonight, he did. Gimme a drink afterwards, too. Let me sit on the veranda till dark, and it was when it was getting dark that I started to think things, wondering, sort of, why he gimme that drink. After he had put me to bed he says I have to take me tablets, as he can tell I'm going to have a bad night if I don't. So I keeps the tablets under me tongue and swallers the water. And then he put the bottle of tablets on the table side of the empty glass, and out he goes with the light. The tablets I spit out and put in me 'jamas' pocket."

"Well, what was wrong with all that?" Bony asked.

"Nuthin', I 'speck. Only that drink, the first one he's given me in years, and leavin' the bottle of tablets on that there little table. He never done that since that time I took two extra to the two Ferris gimme. I was sorta bad that time. They had to get the doctor to me. I thought— I thought——"

"What did you think? Just you tell your old pal."

"I thought—— When I heard that ruddy fowl say: 'Get to hell outa here,' I thought it was Jim come sneakin' home—leavin' his car back on the road a bit, like he's done more'n once. Then I seen you at the winder, and I thought you was 'im. I thought——"

"Well, go on, tell me what you thought."

"I thought he had come back to sneak in on me to see if I'd take any extra tablets."

Bony ignored the implication, saying:

"Pass me your glass. Have another drink. Your nerves are on edge."

"On edge!" echoed the old man. "I'm all in, John Parkes, all in, I tell you, lying here in the dark and thinkin' things and wondering what Jim was doing with that dray. I heard it—in the dark this morning—going away into the scrub. I got to thinking things—how he took the dray into the scrub that morning he said he sacked old Ted O'Brien. Didn't bring it back till high noon, either. You won't tell Jim I tell you things, will you?"

"Hang Jim!" Bony exclaimed somewhat appositely. "Don't worry about me saying anything to him. D'you know why he sent your wife and Ferris to Melbourne?"

"No, but I think things."

"What things?"

"He wants the coast clear to do something or other. Him and Carl Benson. That Carl Benson has made Jim what he is, with his flash cars and flash visitors, and all his brass. Too high and mighty to call in to pass the time of day with me and the old woman. Not like his father. Hey! What about getting a coupler bottles from the spirit store? I got a key. Let's drink and drink, eh?"

"Plenty in this bottle. Did Jim take the women all the way to Melbourne?"

"Took 'em to the railway at Stawell. I heard 'em arguing about not going. They didn't want to go. He made 'em. He makes all of us do what he wants—like he's a sort of officer or something. Gets it from Carl Benson, I says. And from the flashies he takes over to Baden Park at times."

"Rich men, I suppose?"

"Might be. Come here in good cars. Sleeps here most times. Funny about them?"

"What's funny about them?"

"Can't hardly tell. They're different from the ordinary run, what comes to spend the Christmas and Easter. Some of 'em are foreigners too. Cocky lot. Throws out their chests as though they own the Grampians."

"And Jim takes them over to Baden Park. How often do these parties arrive?"

"Not often, but often enough for me. You find out anything about Ted O'Brien?"

"No. D'you think he ever left here?"

The old man caught his breath and then snarled:

"What you wanta ask me that for? How do I know that one?"

"Now don't get off your horse," Bony commanded. "Have another sip. Remember telling me about a man named Bertram, who played the fiddle, with Jim on the organ?"

"Yes. Been here lots of times."

"Did Jim ever take him over to Baden Park?"

"Every time he come. Went over there to play the fiddle to 'em, I suppose. But what's all this got to do with Ted O'Brien?

"Ted O'Brien may have gone over there to work."

"Eh!" exclaimed the old man, and fell silent. Then: "No. No, he wouldn't have gone to Baden Park. Didn't like the present man. But he might have. Cora Benson was always singing out for kitchen help. Servants wouldn't stay account of being too far from the pitcher shows and things."

The invalid fell silent again, and presently Bony asked:

"Is this the only road to Baden Park?"

"The only road now," replied Simpson. "The present man's father drove a track out to the south. Linked up with a track from Moorella to Dunkeld, but avalanches kept blocking it. The present Benson made the road out through here. Spent a lot of money on it too. Done it all back in '45—same year he built that vermin-proof fence."

"Built the road to run that expensive Rolls-Royce on it, eh?"

"No, he did not. He brought that motor-car back with him

when they went to Europe end of '38. Bought them two organs as well, that time, he did. Thousand pounds each he give for 'em. Kurt died in '22, and——"

"Kurt! Who was Kurt?"

"The present man's father, of course. When he died it was found he wasn't as rich as people thought. The present man got going and he made money enough to get himself through the depression, and after that he made it pretty fast. Him and his sister went to Europe in—lemme see—yes, in '35. Then again in '38. Got back just in time to escape the war. Crikey! Him and his sister musta spent a power of brass on traipsing around. Ah! Thanks, my boy. Goo' luck!"

Bony said nothing to interrupt the flow of memory.

"Then the war come and they went quiet. Went on improving the strain of their sheep. After the war they had that there fence put round Baden Park. Ain't never seen it, but I'm told it 'ud keep everything out from an ant to an elephant. They lived quiet, exceptin' for them parties of visitors from the city. Flashies, that's what I say they are. And Jim's like 'em too. Old Kurt Benson was all right. Nothin' flash about him."

"Good friend to you when you first came here, wasn't he?"

"Terrible good, he was. Hadn't been long in Victoria, either."

"When did he settle in Baden Park?"

"Five years afore me. In '07. Come down from New South Wales. Inherited from his father. His father was a vintner, as well as a vineyardist. Name of Schoor."

"Oh! He changed his name, did he?"

"No, his son did—the present man's father changed it to Benson. Old Schoor was a foreigner, if you get me. Swiss or Austrian, I don't know which."

"The present man didn't marry, eh?"

"No, he never married. Neither did his sister, Cora. Got no time for her, John, no ruddy time at all. Times have changed and the new generation's got highfalutin ideas. All they thinks on is getting brass without working for it. What about a drink?"

"There's just one more in the bottle. How are you feeling?"

"Fine, John-oh, fine. Me pains have gone away."

"Think you will sleep now?"

"Why? You leavin' me? You ain't leaving me—not now, are you?"

"Well, I want to have some shut-eye, too, you know."

"But—Jim—he might come back afore daylight."

"If he doesn't he should do," Bony argued. "Now you have this last drink and settle down to sleep."

"Where you goin' to sleep?"

There was wild urgency in his voice, and Bony told him he had made camp in the scrub off the clearing and everything would be all right. That old Simpson was fearful of his son was pathetically evident.

"You bide there, John, just for a little while," pleaded the old man. "Bide there till I sleeps. I ain't feared when you're sitting there in the dark."

"Settle down," Bony said softly. "I'll stay with you."

The invalid sighed, and presently his breathing told of peace. The ethics of giving him drink was not debated by the man who continued to sit on his bed, who sat there until the sound of the Buick reached him. Even then he withdrew only to the fruit trees beyond the veranda, waiting there until assured that James Simpson had gone to his own room.

CHAPTER XXII

SHANNON'S PRIVATE WAR

THERE were, of course, several methods by which to effect entry into Baden Park. One could go through the fence, following the employment of wire-cutters, which Bony did not have with him; one could dig under the fence with a pick and shovel, neither of which tools Bony could carry around; and it was possible to enter by the gate by clinging to the back of Simpson's car when the night was dark. All these methods, however, lacked finesse, and each one would place a limit to visiting the home of Carl Benson, when several visits might be essential.

Bony moved his base of operations to the concealment afforded by seven great boulders closely hemmed in by scrub. Quite close ran a trickling stream and along its borders grass grew green and luscious and much favoured by rabbits, which in turn were favoured by Inspector Napoleon Bonaparte at this particular period.

Less than a hundred yards distant from the boulders ran the great fence, seemingly easily scalable to one who, like Bony, was this evening lying in a declivity near the summit of the tallest boulder. The golden sunlight fell obliquely upon the flat and brilliantly green valley, upon the homestead with its sentinels of trees, the near-by observatory, and upon the ribbon of white road lying straight across the green.

The day was departing when Bony watched Simpson's car speed along the white road and disappear among the homestead trees, and it was gone when with a fire-hardened stick and his hands he began to tunnel under the fence.

To tunnel under the fence was the only way, were he to enter and leave Baden Park when he wished, and the site he chose was where bush debris lay against the barrier and thus offered concealment for both ends of his tunnel. He was compelled to excavate to a depth of three feet and adequately to conceal the earth he removed. When he completed the work day was breaking and his back was breaking, and his hands were torn and painful.

He breakfasted on grilled rabbit and a crust of damper, and there would be no more bread, because there remained no more flour. There was no more tobacco, either, but he did have a store of cigarette-ends and about twenty matches, a fistful of tea and a little sugar.

He slept through the day till shortly before five o'clock, when leisurely he brewed a pot of tea and ate the remainder of the rabbit. He planned that night to investigate the homestead and those who lived there, and he was with deliberate unhaste drawing at a cigarette when he heard the sound of shooting. There were four reports, to him being no louder than a cork drawn from a bottle.

Within the space of five seconds he was high in the niche near the summit of the tallest boulder and directing his gaze towards the homestead. He could see the golden discs of oranges, but nothing that moved in the vicinity of the house and observatory. He could actually see the blue smoke rising lazily from one of the three chimneys. Then again he heard the shooting, a fraction more distinctly, but not nearer, and coming from the range at his back.

Several minutes edged by him, and then he heard two further reports, followed after a short interval by one. When no additional reports reached him he decided to investigate what were obviously the reports of a rifle or rifles.

Then he heard the aeroplane.

It was high up and approaching from the west, a pencil of gold which grew wings prior to circling the homestead. A machine of medium size, it landed in a paddock skirted by the creek and taxied towards the homestead like a cicada first trying its wings. A man appeared outside the garden hedge and walked forward to greet three people who alighted from the machine.

It was evident to Bony that the people at the homestead had not heard the shooting, and the shooting submerged the interest aroused by the advent of the visitors to Baden Park. He considered it probable that the shots had been fired in Shannon's private war, because it was most unlikely that sportsmen would be shooting kangaroos or wallabies or wild dogs. Damn Shannon, if he were the cause of the firing, and thus almost certain to stir up a hornets' nest when it was vital that the hornets should remain quiescent.

He began the long ascent of the mountain back, which ended in the precipice overlooking Baden Park Hotel, feeling annoyance, yet doubly cautious.

On reaching the crest, he moved slowly parallel with it for a quarter of a mile before going down the slope almost at right angles. Half-way down, a flash of colour sent him to earth. It kept him there for some time. The colour had been light brown, and he was puzzled because the birds in the vicinity were not alarmed. On again, in action not unlike an iguana, he had proceeded only a dozen yards when he saw a saddled horse anchored to the ground by its trailing reins. Several minutes lapsed before he crawled a little nearer, to be halted once more by the sight of the rider.

If the man was "foxing" he was doing it remarkably well, so well, in fact, that the birds were not taking the slightest interest in him and giving all their attention to Bony. The man lay upon his back several yards from his horse, one hand clutching a rifle, the other resting high up on his chest.

Assured now that the man was dead, Bony went forward, foot by foot, the horse now facing him with its ears pricked. Then Bony sighed with the resignation of the martyr, for buried in the rider's throat was a throwing knife.

Tragedy was written clearly on this page of the Book of the Bush, and Bony could have read it easily enough had not caution demanded the harder way. Instead of going directly forward he had to encircle the man and horse, still on hands and knees, until finally he read a paragraph.

Two riders had been travelling together from the east, from the road to Dunkeld, from which they might have set out. One had drawn his rifle from its scabbard and had received a knife in his throat, and the other had ridden down the slope and not towards the Station gate.

Bony followed the tracks of the second horse, relying on the birds and his eyesight to warn him of a waiting enemy, often halting to sniff the breeze and to listen, although the wind was coming from behind and of little assistance.

Then he saw the second horse. It was gazing down the slope, curiosity its master. The reins had been slipped from its head, the loop tossed over the broken limb of a low tree. A brown fantail was dancing on the pommel of the saddle.

Determining the point at which the horse was seeing or hearing something invisible to him, Bony began a wide detour, hoping that the animal would not betray his presence by whinnying. Five minutes later he saw the second man. He was lying on his chest, as though sighting his rifle round the bulge of a boulder, and, like the first, he was dressed as a stockman.

The stalking Bonaparte cut Shannon's tracks, and the tracks revealed that the American had been running in zigzag fashion when the second rider went to earth. That he had died whilst sighting along the rifle was proven by the red bar of colour joining his face to the ground, but Bony could not decide how, whether by knife or bullet, as he dared not approach too close.

Now, on Shannon's tracks, he saw that the American had been racing for the cover provided by a lone granite monolith poised so acutely that it was astonishing the wind didn't topple it over. Distance from the second dead man, as well as the position of the dead man, told that Shannon had killed him from the cover of this column of granite, and Bony could not be confident that the American was not still behind it and still full of sting, engrossed by his private war to the extent of shooting at sight. The silly thought flared through Bony's mind that it would be just damned stupid for a married man with responsibilities to be shot dead by an ally.

Further detouring was, therefore, clearly indicated. He found Shannon seated on the ground and with his back resting against the monolith. His eyes were closed and he could have been asleep, were it not for the narrow rivulet of congealed blood giving his right temple and cheek the appearance of being split open. Resting on his lap and grasped by his right hand was the pistol with the silencer attachment.

Slowly Bony crept towards him, intent on possessing himself of the pistol and undecided whether Shannon was sleeping or unconscious.

Shannon was neither unconscious nor asleep. He was feeling sick. The ache of his head was something to remember for many years, and he had to be still and keep his eyes closed. He heard no sound, but instinct warned him. He opened one eye with an effort and then the other. He stared into blazing blue eyes in a dark face less than six inches beyond his feet. A dark hand was thrust forward towards his pistol. Bony said politely:

"Good evening!"

CHAPTER XXIII

BONY'S DISPATCH

GLEN SHANNON touched his head wound, looked at his fingers, and registered slight disappointment that red blood was not smeared on them. His eyes held pain, but his voice was as whimsical as usual.

"Had the idea I was cracked by a bullet," he drawled. "Certainly had that idea. Musta been a meteor."

"Bullet all right," snapped Bony, sitting back on his heels and resting against the monolith beside the American. "It creased the right side of your head. How d'you feel?"

"Pretty wild, Bony, old pal. I knew there was something I forgot to buy me at Dunkeld. Now I know. I forgot to include aspirin when I laid in them stores. How come?"

"Tell me what happened," commanded Bony, and Shannon's underlip was thrust outward rebelliously, then was sucked back. The voice, the intensity of the blue eyes which he encountered quelled him when guns had failed. "How many horsemen were there?"

Shannon groaned. "Only two," he replied. "I was a bit careless with the second hombre. Having been mooching around most of last night, I decided I'd camp and I chose a place between two stone slabs. That was early this morning, and I slept good and sound until a crow somewhere handy woke me with his cawing. Instead of waking up properly, I mumbled a curse or two and drifted off again. Then I heard a guy say: 'Hi, you!' and I sits up and sees two characters on horses, and one of 'em looking down at me over his rifle sights. They weren't nice characters, not like you, Bony. They had a mean look about 'em, and when they tell me to stand up and reach for the sky, I slips a knife into my hand as I'm scrambling to my feet.

"I'm not at all pleased with that crow who musta give me away to these characters, and the one aiming the rifle tells the other one to dismount and come up behind to search me for weapons, as the guy is getting off his horse, and the other guy is saying how pleased he is to meet up with me after I had refused to stay and drink with him that night I left the hotel, I recalls what Pa advised to do in a situation like this. So I sorta stared at a bush behind him and nodded slightly, and that caused him to relax a trifle and so—take the knife.

"The other guy dives behind a rock with his rifle, and as I'm in the open, I can't pause to talk to him. He shoots twice as I'm on my way, but I'm not travelling in the same direction more'n one second at a time, and the only shooting he's ever done has been on a rifle-range. To be real tough, a guy has to be fast, and me, I was fast, having been brought up that way. The second guy wasted time getting on his horse again. I got a good lead, but he soon reduced it and slid off his horse and did his stuff. I quite enjoyed the noise he made, and he wasn't doing me any harm until I was sorta careless. He nipped me above the ear with a bullet, according to you, and while I was drifting into slumber I finished the war as far as he was concerned. You know how 'tis. A guy can be easily bumped off when he's unconscious."

Shannon having finished speaking, Bony made no comment as he was summing up the action and trying to assess its likely results.

"You can't blame me, Bony, old pal," Shannon went on. "I didn't start the war, honour bright. There was me, lying comfortably asleep. I wasn't sleeping on no private property, like Baden Park."

"Where did you leave your pack?" Bony cut in.

"Where? Now lemme think. Where did I leave that pack?"

"Take it easy," Bony ordered. "I'll go after those horses. We must get away from here. I have work for you to accomplish tonight."

Shannon rested his head upon his folded arms and thus did not see Bony's departure in the gloom to stalk the dead men and relieve the bodies of identification documents and, with the assurance he did not feel, collect the horses and bring them to the monolith. Shannon was ordered to mount, and in single file Bony led the way eastward and then down off the range to stop only at a shallow but swift-running creek. He watered the horses whilst the American stepped into the water, knelt in the stream, and laved his aching head.

"Can you remember now where you left your pack?" he asked when Shannon joined him and said that the icy water had given relief.

"No, I can't—not yet. It's mighty peculiar, not remembering. But I will."

"Had you seen either of those two men before today?"

"Yes, both of 'em at the saloon several times. One of them arrived in the car that night I left, as I told you. They're Baden Park sheep-herders."

"And do you remember that one of them pointed a rifle at you and told you to get up and raise your arms?"

"A guy can forget where he left his wallet or his watch, or even his pack, but he don't forget looking into a rifle-barrel," replied the American seriously.

"What have you been doing since that morning Simpson burned the body?"

"Mooching around some. I saw a truck deliver beer and stores at the hotel and take on stores and petrol to Baden Park. It didn't come back. The driver was one of Benson's herders. I saw Simpson leave the hotel with his mother and Ferris and return in three hours. That's about all."

"H'm! D'you know where we are?"

Shannon gazed at the mountain crest supporting the sky in which still remained a little light.

"Guess we're not so far from the Dunkeld road," he replied.

"We are about a mile from it. Do you think you could locate your bike?"

"Sure. It'll be safe enough."

"You are going to set off for Dunkeld right away," Bony stated. "You are going to take a message from me to the policeman stationed there. After you have delivered the message you may return and carry on with your war, because you cannot be more deeply sunk than you are for having killed two Australian stockmen."

"Say——" Shannon began, and was cut off.

"It ought not to take more than an hour to reach Dunkeld on your machine," Bony continued firmly. "Another hour to return makes it only two hours away from the battlefield. You can easily spare me that little period of time, and I know you will most gladly do so. Have you ever considered the possibility that your sweetheart may be alive?"

"No!" The word was flung at Bony, and to his forearm was clamped a vice of flesh and bone. "What d'you know, Bony, old pal? Come on, tell a guy—quick."

"I know nothing, and because her body has not been found, I refuse to believe that she is dead. Therefore, I proceed on the assumption that she's alive. It is a possibility which we must accept, and so have to use our brains with greater facility than we use our pistols and our knives. You were in the Army, and you must appreciate the relationship of an army to its general. I have elected myself the general because it is the general's task to think. I want two hours of your time. Do I get it?"

Shannon said: "You do," and added nothing.

They mounted and rode forward in the dark, and Shannon gave proof of his bushmanship by sighting the ranges against the sky so that when they reached the road it was within half a mile of his hidden motor-cycle. As the American was removing the waterproof sheeting from it, Bony asked:

"What is your opinion of those two riders? D'you think they were sent out to locate you?"

"No. I reckon they happened to be passing and the crow roused their suspicions."

"I think you're right," Bony said. "They must have come from the east, otherwise I would have crossed their tracks when I went up the slope to investigate. They could have been returning from Dunkeld, taking a short cut to the entrance gate instead of following the road round past the hotel."

He assisted the American to push the machine to the road, confident that the noise of its engine would be beaten off from the hotel by the wind blowing lazily from the north. Shannon bestrode the machine, started and warmed the engine, and then cut it dead at Bony's command.

"I must write a little note," Bony said. "We will sit at the side of the road and you shall strike matches to give me light."

The note was written in three minutes, sealed in an envelope, and handed to the American.

"You have to contact Constable Groves without any delay. If he is out of town on duty, you must still contact him and give this report. He will at once proceed to Glenthompson because the telephone system in this district may be, shall we say, defective. From Glenthompson he will contact Inspector Mulligan at Ballarat. He will inform Mulligan that I request the arrest of both Simpson and Benson for the murder of Edward O'Brien and that I require a large party to raid Baden Park. He will also inform Mulligan that you will be waiting at the entrance gate to Baden Park Station to give him further information. Is that clear?"

"Yes."

"Having given the note to Constable Groves, you will return to this place, park your machine in the scrub, and mount the horse I will leave tethered close by. You will then ride to those locked gates inside which Simpson burned the body. Take with you a spanner to remove the bolted hinges, the size of the nuts being one inch and a half. By removing the hinges of one gate you will be able to draw both gates clear of the road and thus leave it open for Mulligan. Then you will wait for Mulligan at the electrically controlled main gate, and on his arrival, if I am not with you, you will inform him that I am at the homestead and that he is to take the place by storm and arrest everyone on sight. Is that clear too?"

"Clear as battery water, Bony, old pal, but——"

"Well?"

"When ought the cops to arrive at the main gate?"

"Before daybreak. I shall be counting on that hour. You will do nothing whatever to upset the peace of the summer night—and should you find it necessary to take action to preserve the peace of the summer night you will do so discreetly. Remember that you have already shot one man and knifed another. Remember, too, the most important factor is that swift and silent approach by the police might well be vital to the safety of your sweetheart and her friend—if they still live. Now get along and don't spare the horses."

When the noise of Shannon's machine faded into the silence beyond the sound of the slight wind in the trees, Bony was smoking a cigarette and reading the papers he had taken from the bodies of the stockmen, reading with the aid of a small fire carefully hidden in dense scrub. He learned that the name of one was Paul Lartz, a Czechoslovakian subject naturalised in 1938, and the other was named William Spicer, according to a letter addressed by Bertram & Company, Melbourne, who stated that letters received for Spicer would be forwarded to Baden Park. There was a second letter forwarded by Bertram & Company from a man signing himself Hans Stromberg. It was dated June 11, 1946, from a P.O.W. camp north of Victoria, the writer expressing fervent hopes of being soon returned to Germany.

The camp, Bony recalled, confined German soldiers found to be dangerous members of the Nazi party.

Germans and Germany! How often had some association with Germany cropped up in this investigation! Doubtless Spicer was an alias for a German. Bertram was a German name. In fact, Bertram was a German. The Czech could be a Sudeten German. Then there were the Bensons, whose father's name was Schoor, said by old Simpson to have been Austrian or Swiss. Organs from Germany. Ah! And stockmen who rode like soldiers and who gave careless salutes which could be the Nazi salutes carefully disguised.

The Bensons had been in Germany in 1939. Through the war years they had worked and lived quietly and had made money. In '45 they had made the new road over the mountain and past the hotel to the Dunkeld road. After the war, after '45, they had entertained parties of people said by old Simpson to be unlike the type of visitors who toured the Grampians and stayed at the hotel over Christmas and Easter, parties who "throw out their chests like they own the Grampians." Germans!

It was a thoughtful man who rode in the dark over bad country to the hidden camp amid the boulders at that place he had burrowed under the great fence. There he ate the remainder of his cooked food and smoked two cigarettes from the last of his preserved ends.

Ten minutes later he was standing inside the fence. He looked at the stars. It wanted two minutes till ten-thirty.

CHAPTER XXIV

REBELS IN WHITE

MINUS the heavy swag and gunny-sack, Bony travelled light and fast, keeping parallel with the fence to reach the gate and follow the road. The night was dark though the stars were clear, and he did not see the wire over which he almost tripped. It had been dragged away from the fence after a repair job, but it was still tough and flexible.

He had left it behind when an idea halted him, sent him back to break off about four feet of it by constantly bending and opening the bend. One end of the broken-off piece he bent into a long hook, slipped the hook down through his belt, from which it was suspended something like a sword. A length of heavy wire is a handy weapon against men and dogs.

The gate was shut, but it opened when he stood on the metal bar inset into the roadway. It closed again shortly after he removed his weight. He thought of placing a boulder on the bar to keep the gate open for Mulligan and discarded the idea because someone arriving or departing before he was ready would give the alarm.

Keeping well off the road, Bony arrived eventually at an open gateway in a massive hedge guarded by a plain wire fence, and because the wind was coming from the north and there being the likelihood of dogs, he skirted the hedge to the south and so came to the anchored aeroplane and the wicket gate through which the passengers had been conducted.

Beyond the wicket gate and through the short tunnel in the hedge was the house, several of its rooms being brilliantly illuminated. To the left of the house was the observatory. The men's quarters and the outbuildings must be situated on the far side.

Having unlaced his boots and hidden them in the hedge, he made his way through the garden and on to the lawn laid before the front of the house, moving like a wisp of fog in a lightless dungeon.

The house was the usual bungalow type and built three feet above ground, this side being skirted by a wide veranda having four steps to it along its entire length. From the lawn it was not possible to see the lower portion of the rooms beyond the open french windows.

Bony spent five minutes assuring himself that none other was in the garden, and then he slipped along the black bar between two of the broad ribbons of light falling half-way across the lawn, to float up the veranda steps and gain the shadow against the wall between two pairs of windows. The murmur of voices rose to clarity as he edged one eye round a window frame.

The size of the room, the electroliers, the tapestries on the walls, the long table of gleaming walnut, the floor covering, the high-backed chairs; the two women and the twelve men seated at the table, the sergeant-major of a butler, and the huge portrait against the end wall, all comprised but a hazy background to the presentation of two young women arrayed entirely in white.

Seated at the head of the table was the man who had watched the burning of O'Brien's body. At the far end of the table sat the man who had conveyed the body on the dray. Upon Benson's right hand and on his left sat a woman, middle-aged but preserved by all the arts, big-framed, and stiff. Like Benson and James Simpson, the other men were in formal evening clothes. Directed by the butler, the two women in white served the host and his guests.

The conversation was conducted in a language with which Bony was unfamiliar. It was a harsh, masculine tongue, and the men and women who spoke it were masculine and harsh and handsomely arrogant. They sat stiffly, moved jerkily, like subalterns at mess when the general is present. No one smiled. They were of one race, blond and square. The men looked corseted, save Simpson, who was not of them.

The serving maids! One was a brunette, slim and pretty. The other's hair gleamed like the aftermath of a sunset. She was taller than her companion and more robust. She was worth any young man's voyage across the world.

It had been logical to assume that these two young women had wandered off the road and had perished in the bush. It had been logical to assume that they had been murdered because they had stumbled upon a dreadful crime or a tremendous secret. It had been logical even to assume that they had been kidnapped to appease the hunger of lascivious brutes, but to have been kidnapped into domestic service Bony had not permitted himself to assume.

Domestic service in Australia, even in this ultra-democratic age, is not impossible to obtain. The Bensons possessed the wherewithal to induce girls from Dunkeld, and even Melbourne, to come to Baden Park. Why, then, kidnap two tourists and compel them to domestic service? Why, when such an act, if discovered, would surely ruin them?

When discovered! Perhaps it had never been intended that it be discovered.

That these two girls had been kidnapped was surely true because they had not been seen after they left the hotel; they had not communicated with their parents and friends since leaving Dunkeld. That they had been impressed into domestic service was only too obvious, for rebellion was in both faces and even in the manner in which they walked to and from the serving bench.

Their fate was plain enough now. Old Simpson and Carl Benson between them had drawn the picture. James Simpson had known that the Bensons could not employ domestic servants because of something they had to keep hidden. Benson had referred to surrendering to his sister's demand. So James Simpson had brought the two hotel guests at Baden Park to be inspected by Cora Benson, to be approved of by her, to be claimed by her from her brother, who had engineered the kidnapping.

They three, the Bensons, brother and sister, and Simpson, were *au fait* with this crime upon the persons of two Australian women, and the other woman and the other ten men must also be *au fait* with it.

But why? Why kidnap these two girls? Why murder the old yardman? Why slay Detective Price? Why insult or assault hotel guests? Why shoot it out with Glen Shannon, who had every legal and moral right to be where he was bailed up? Who and what were these people who did these things? What was their secret, to preserve which a man and a woman of wealth and social position connived at murder?

Benson had spoken of a trust, even as the remains of an old

160

yardman were being cremated. A trust! How much did those two press-ganged girls know of it? If they knew nothing of it, they were still press-ganged, still the turnkeys to open the door of a gaol to receive Carl and Cora Benson. How would they fare at the hands of these people when Mulligan and his men arrived?

The thrill of achievement coursed hotly through the veins of the watching Bonaparte. When a police organisation had turned its attention to other matters for want of clues, he had undertaken the assignment to bring to light the fate of two young women who had disappeared in the bush five months previously. He could reveal their fate, but he yet had to prove it, to do which he must produce the bodies before persons able to identify them.

At the first sign of an invasion by Mulligan, these women might be whisked away beyond reach. They might be taken in the aeroplane, flown over the not-distant sea, and jettisoned with weights attached to them. At all costs he would have to get them out of the house and into a place of safety before Mulligan's police cars skidded to a stop at the front door.

Instinctively he glanced round to observe the time-telling stars, found he could see none beyond the arc of diffused light, swiftly essayed the guess that it must be eleven-thirty. A peculiar hour for people to be seated before a meal comprising several courses. The food and drink being served recalled to him the hunger he was experiencing, the hunger created by a sharply unbalanced diet. Yet there was no envy in him, none of the despair of one on the outside looking in, for within the fine apartment the atmosphere was so foreign to ordinary human conviviality that he was chilled by it.

Not once had anyone smiled. Carl Benson did most of the talking. Once Simpson spoke to his left-hand neighbour, asking in English what the passenger load of the aeroplane was, and was told "eight", in so brusque a manner that his face became faintly flushed. Everyone was on edge, as though facing a momentous decision or a tremendous event.

Then happened that which made Bony fighting mad and yet glad that Shannon was not with him.

Red Head was pouring wine into the glass before the woman facing the windows, who was clearly the sister of Carl Benson, when the woman's arm inadvertently came into contact with

161

the napkined bottle. The result—a little wine upon the polished table. Red Head straightened up, and the woman, with no expression upon her large face and no detectable alteration of expression in her eyes, raised her hand and slapped the girl's face.

Before the sound of the blow ceased its echo down the corridors of Bony's mind, the butler was behind Red Head, one great hand fastened about her hand clasping the bottle. She was snatched away from the table as though she were a feather duster and whisked to the serving bench, where her other arm was swept up her back in a half nelson and the bottle removed from her right hand.

No one at the table turned his head or removed his gaze from Carl Benson, and Benson did not pause for a fraction in what he was saying. The butler, six feet two and weighing in the vicinity of fifteen stone of everything bar fat, placed the bottle on the serving bench, released his hold of the arm behind the girl's back, and violently pushed her against the wall. Then he marched to the table, swabbed up the spilled wine, and proceeded to fill the woman's glass.

Red Head didn't cry. She stood beside the serving bench, hands clenched, green eyes blazing, chest heaving. Her fellow-servant left the board with used plates, and as she crossed to the bench she shook her head, imploring Red Head to do nothing. Then, astoundingly, the butler marched to the serving bench, took a bottle from an ice-pail, withdrew the cork, wrapped the bottle, and presented it to Red Head. Red Head returned to the table to continue serving.

The meal came to an end. The remnants of the meal were transferred to the serving bench by the two girls, the butler assisting. At an order from him, Red Head passed out of the room, to reappear beyond the shutter which opened behind the bench. She drew out the loaded trays passed to her by the butler, and the brunette left the room. The shutter was closed and the butler fastened it. Then he locked the door and proceeded to serve wine in fresh glasses, the diners remaining seated and silent.

Every glass charged, the butler took up the glass he had filled for himself and stood beside Benson. Benson looked up at him standing as stiffly as the best of sergeant-majors, and then he, too, rose to his feet, followed by the company.

A guest began to speak. He was tall, lean, grey, and soldierly in bearing. He spoke in the same language, keeping his light blue eyes directed at a point just above the opposite man's head. The others became statues, each of them holding the wineglass poised at a level with his or her face. The toast, for it was certainly that, was a long one. The voice was low but loaded with emotion, so much so that Bony, who could not understand a word, felt it powerfully.

Abruptly the voice ceased its outpouring. The ensuing silence could be measured. Benson spoke the same word twice, and in time with the third utterance of the word the company gave a single great shout. Glasses were drained and then cascaded into the great Benares bowl upon the table.

The melodrama thrilled Bony down to the soles of his naked feet.

The butler stalked to the door and, unlocking it, threw it open. The company almost stalked, too, as they drifted out of the room. And then Bony was off the veranda, crouching down beyond its edge as he watched the butler close and fasten the windows and finally switch off the lights.

Continuing to feel the peculiar emotional reaction to the voice of the toast giver and the final smashing of the glasses, Bony debated his next step. He toyed with the idea of testing the french windows to gain entry to the house, gave that away and decided to reconnoitre outside the building and familiarise himself with the set-up of the homestead.

It was important to locate where the hands were quartered and their approximate number. It was vitally important to have the entire plan of the place in his mind that he might move quickly if speed of action was essential. That done, he could proceed to contact the girls and get them out of the house and into a place of safety. They had to come first, and of that there could be no argument.

The languorous wind whispered to the orange trees and the smaller shrubs. The stars gleamed like sequins on a woman's velvet dress. A black and shapeless shape moved swiftly along the darkened side of the house, passed round it, flitted on to pause before a lighted window, broke into rapid movement, and slipped up into a flowering gum tree. From the gum tree Bony could gaze into a large kitchen.

Both girls had changed into blue linen house-frocks. One

was polishing glasses, the other washing dishes. They were talking and they were alone. They talked without smiling and yet without sulkiness. Red Head was still indignant, Brunette still pleading.

Bony had yet to master the plan of the homestead, but he was tempted to knock upon the window and urge the girls to escape with him. The opportunity, however, although appearing favourable, was not felt to be so in view of all the other aspects of this new development.

Having finished the chores, the girls came to stand near the window, where they linked arms as though gaining comfort by the affectionate contact, talking earnestly, the one soothing the outraged nerves of the other. They stood thus for several moments, when the butler appeared, armed with an oversize flashlight.

Beckoning with his head, he marched out, followed by the girls.

Bony dropped lightly from the tree, hope given him by the flashlight carried by the butler. The shapeless shape danced away from the kitchen window, withdrew a little farther from the house, stopped beyond the next corner that two sides of the house could be watched.

A door was opened on that side opposite to the lawn, and a man issued from it, closing the door behind him. Bony went to ground, searched for, found a sky-line. Along the sky-line he observed the head and shoulders of James Simpson, and Simpson crossed a wide, gravelled space and entered the dark observatory. The next moment a light appeared in a small window high from the ground.

Immediately the light had been switched on inside the observatory, another house door was opened and three figures issued from it. This time, across Bony's sky-line slid the heads and shoulders of the two girls, followed by that of the butler. His flashlight came on, the beam aimed steadily at the ground about the girls' feet as they walked over open gravelled space, skirted the observatory, and halted before the door of a small building. After them, like a long-legged tiger cat, skipped Inspector Bonaparte.

CHAPTER XXV

THE OPENING SCORE

Twice the butler raised the angle of his flashlight, revealing to Bony that they were crossing a wide gravelled area hemmed by the house, the observatory, the outbuildings, and the stacks of fodder. It was obvious that the two girls had taken this little journey before, because, without direction from their escort, they walked straight to one of the outbuildings.

Before the door of this building they stopped and the man passed them, to throw his light upon the lock, which he proceeded to free. The door was pushed inward. The girls entered, an interior light was switched on, and the butler then relocked the door. When he stalked back to the house, Bony was lying full length at the base of the observatory.

The man having entered the house, Bony crossed to the outbuildings. It was constructed of stone blocks, and it needed no light to inform him that the door was heavy and solid and that it was secured by a bolt kept in place by a padlock of the Yale type.

He could hear the murmuring voices of the inmates, and without making his presence known to them, he circled the building, and so arrived below a small window set high in the wall. The window was open, and the light within revealed thick iron bars bisecting it. Here the voices were louder but the words indistinguishable.

Bony waited until the light went out, and then, reaching up, he began to tap a tattoo upon the window-sill. When nothing happened he so employed his wire sword as the drumstick, and then above the soft tapping came a voice asking who it was.

"A friend," he called softly. "Don't put on the light."

He jumped and caught hold of the lowest bar, pulling himself upward so that his face was above the sill. He could feel the warmth of the room. A vague shape moved just beyond the bars and the sound of quick breathing played upon his ears.

"Are you Mavis Sanky and Beryl Carson?" he whispered.

An exclamation, and then steadily:

"Yes. Who are you? What do you want?"

"Well, for one thing, I want to get you out. I presume you would like to be free. As I told you, I'm a friend—and a policeman. I want you to answer my questions as shortly as possible because time is vital."

"All right."

"Tell me how many hands are employed here?"

"Seven."

"Whereabouts are they quartered, do you know?"

"Two, no, three buildings from here. On my right. But they'll be over at the house with the Bensons and their visitors."

"The hands were not at table with the company this evening?" Bony queried.

"Oh yes, they were. All of them excepting the two who are away. They're not real stockmen."

"I didn't think so. When are the absent two expected back, d'you know?"

"Tonight," replied a different voice. "I heard Heinrich ask Mr. Benson, and he said they should have been back from Dunkeld before it was dark. They're not stockmen, as Mavis said. They're all foreigners, excepting the Bensons and that man from the hotel."

"And you were abducted, were you not?"

"Yes," indignantly. "They were waiting for us on the road —after we left the hotel. They forced us into a car and we fought them, so they chloroformed us or something. The last thing I remember was seeing that old yardman at the hotel looking out from behind some bushes. We were brought here and compelled to work for Miss Benson."

"We refused, of course," said the other girl, and when Bony asked what then happened, her voice was vibrant with anger. "They whipped us. They tied our hands together round a post. She was there and counted the strokes. Heinrich did it with a whip with lots of thongs on it. Ten strokes that woman counted for each of us. We went on strike again a few weeks after that and got fifteen strokes that time. We daren't refuse to work after that, scrubbing and washing and waiting at table for the beasts."

"Oh, please get us out of here. Smash the door down or something."

"No, Beryl, not that. They would hear. Mister—out there— you might get the key of the door bolt. It's hanging on a nail just inside the side door."

"The door by which you left the house?" Bony asked.

"Yes, that's the door. Will you try to get it?"

"I won't *try* to get it," Bony said. "I'll just get it. Now you dress and wait for me. I may not return for an hour, but be patient. Now tell me. What's going on here?"

"We don't know. It's something inside the observatory. They hold a kind of service over there, generally at night. They're going to have a service tonight. Yes, there's the organ."

"Who attends the service?"

"Everyone who's here."

"What about this Heinrich man?"

"Oh, he goes too. Serves them with drinks and refreshments."

"How long does the service continue?" Bony pressed.

"Two hours at least. Sometimes much longer."

"You don't know what kind of service?"

"Can't even guess. That hotel man plays the organ, and sometimes someone or other sings. It's all foreign to us."

"All right," Bony whispered. "Now I'll be going. Dress in the dark and be ready. Have you your walking-shoes?"

"No. They took our shoes from us the day after they brought us here. Shoes! It'll be weeks before we can wear shoes again after having had to wear slippers for months."

Hands reached forward and became clasped over Bony's hands gripping the bars.

"You'll take care, won't you?"

Bony chuckled encouragingly, and he said with a confidence he dared not mistrust:

"Don't you worry. I'll be all right. Anyway, there's a friend of mine not very far away. I wonder if you know him. Which of you is Mavis Sanky?"

The hands upon his own pressed hard, and their owner gave the affirmative reply.

"His name is Glen Shannon."

"Glen!" almost shouted the girl, and her friend hushed her

and cried: "You always said your American would come looking for you, didn't you?"

"Well, he has been looking for you, and you will see him soon. So both be good girls and obey orders, and don't switch on your light or make any noise. I'll get that key, but it may take time. Au revoir!"

Relaxing his grip, he dropped to the ground, picked up the wire, and passed round to the front of the building.

Opposite was the observatory, two wide windows set very wide apart appearing as the eyes of a pagan idol emitting music instead of fire. To the left, the house, with its main entrance illumined by a porch light. The side door was open and he could see a small hall beyond.

Once again the shapeless shape danced through the corridors of the night. Bony located the hands' quarters, a spacious building and empty of light. His nose located the paint and oil stores, and fire was the natural idea-association with oil. The door being unlocked, he entered, and with his fingers found a tapped drum of kerosene and an empty bucket which he filled from the drum. Diversionary tactics are easily executed, and with greater celerity, by the application of kerosene and a lighted match to a fodder stack.

One of the stacks was of oats, and it had been broken open. Loose straw was there, which he piled against the open cut and saturated with the kerosene. The ignited match could be applied if and when events decided the moment.

Everything he saw, even in the darkness, bespoke the wealth and the prosperity of the owner of Baden Park. There was no litter. Somewhere in the distance, removed that its noise would not disturb, hummed a powerful generating plant. The garage building contained seven stalls, each having an automatic door, whilst under one great iron roof was enough machinery to work a dozen ordinary farms.

Satisfied that he was now familiar with the scene of the probable battle to come, Bony drifted back to the observatory and discovered several points of interest. The building was square in shape, its thirty-feet high walls of granite blocks supporting the cupola, and its only doorway facing towards the house. The door was ajar. It was almost four inches thick and was fitted with heavy iron hinges reaching almost across its width, like the door of an old church. There was no keyhole and no fastening bolt. Near the left-hand corner a series of iron rungs gave access to the cupola, Bony assuming that when the telescope was installed certain mechanism required periodic attention.

As though to a time-table, people appeared in the main doorway of the house, and Bony skipped to the far side of the observatory and peered round the wall angle to watch the house party arrive. They walked slowly and solemnly, as people walk to church. The butler pushed open the door, stood aside, then went in last. The door was partly closed, leaving a five-inch ribbon of light to fall upon the ground.

The music faded into silence, and the enthralled Bony could hear the subdued voices within. They went on for perhaps a minute, when the organist began again to play and Heinrich emerged and went back to the house, where he switched off the exterior light over the main door, closed that door, and passed to the secondary or side door. Bony could see him cross what appeared to be a small hall and disappear beyond.

The organ produced sound like the wind in faraway trees, rising and falling, and gradually gaining in strength until it became the rolling drums of a funeral march.

He was tempted to steal to the door and peer within. What he might see was tearing his patience to shreds, but he could not risk discovery until he had removed the imprisoned girls to safety. He recognised the influence of the music, the stirring of his pulses, the arousing of emotion at the cost of caution. Himself no musician, he had to offer silent tribute to the organist, for the music was claiming him, touching him with its magic fingers, removing control of imagination.

The influence of the music was such that he did not see Heinrich until the butler had left the house, leaving the side door open, and was half-way to the observatory door. And then, instead of waiting, immediately the man had entered the observatory, Bony ran to the side door, turned to see if he had been observed, and went in through the doorway back first, snatching the key hanging from the nail.

Movement in the small hall spun him round to face a man who had entered from the passage beyond and now stood with astonishment in his steel-blue eyes at sight of the tattered and bootless Bonaparte. A yard only separated them.

Bony's reactions came in sequence. First a feeling of annoyance with himself at not counting the men who had entered the observatory, for this man must have been one of the round dozen he had seen at table. Then followed the feeling of frustration, for, although he had the key, there was still the prison door to be opened without being observed, and other matters to attend to without his presence being noted. Nothing could be permitted to thwart the success of his plans.

The man regarding Bony was distinctly hostile. He took one pace nearer to him, and his right hand flashed upward into the left-hand side of his evening jacket. Voluntary action with him then ceased. The wire sword hissed and fell across his exposed wrist. He staggered back, raised his head to shout, and so exposed his throat to the bite of the wire.

There was no scream. Bony had him in his arms before he could collapse to the floor.

CHAPTER XXVI

THE ''CURTAIN''

GIVEN additional strength by the thought of the imminent return of Heinrich, he carried the body along the passage, stopped before one of the doors, opened it, and took the body into the dark interior of the room. He could hear the butler's tread in the small hall, and he heard the man's footsteps in the passage as without sound he closed the door.

The footsteps passed. In darkness Bony crouched over the dead man and relieved the body of a small-calibre automatic and a bulky pocket wallet, which he stowed inside his shirt. He found a bed, and under the bed he pushed the body.

The lowest notes of the organ reached him even there. They were like the slow heart-beats of a dying man. He thought of the organist, of the persons listening to the organ, of the two girls who had been flogged into domestic service, of two milk-white backs bloodied and scarred for life. He thought of Benson, cold, hard, and rigid, and of his sister, stiff and merciless.

The butler passed along the passage to the small hall, and Bony opened the bedroom door and peered round the frame to see the man leave the house. Slipping into the passage and closing the door, he raced to the hall, and from round the frame of the outer door watched the butler cross and enter the observatory. Twenty seconds later he was unlocking the padlock securing the bolt of the prison door.

The door was opened before he could push it inward, and the girls emerged to stand close to him, to touch him as though belief was impossible that he was their rescuer.

"It's a fine night for a stroll, among other things," he told them. "Are you ready?"

He commanded them not to speak and to walk as softly as possible on the gravel. The organist was playing something with an extraordinary throb in it, and as they moved away from the prison a woman's voice broke into song. Bony's pulses had been stirred, but this song stirred them in another way. She sang superbly, and stone walls could not distort her voice, rich and full, and giving the promise of all delights.

Bony expelled his breath and, taking the girls by the arm, he drew them away, passing the house, reaching the open gateway in the encircling hedge, and so to the road. And in his heart a pang of regret that he could not stay and listen to the singer.

He had succeeded in the most difficult part of the operation, which, however, was uncompleted. There was the key in his pocket, and it ought to be on its nail inside the doorway. Its position had been prominent, and Heinrich might well miss it despite the fact that familiar objects, or absence of them, are unregistered by a mind occupied with an important event.

The thought switched his mind to another track. Why go back to the homestead? Once again he had finalised a case he had consented to accept. He had been asked to establish the fate of two missing girls, and now he had done just that to his own satisfaction. It remained for him to get them clear of Baden Park and into the hands of people who knew them, or the police, when their story could be told to the world's satisfaction. He had laboured and suffered hardship, both physical and mental, and the cleaning of this nest of murderers and abductors would rightly be the task for Mulligan.

Was it not his duty to guard these two girls until the police arrived? Well? Perhaps; perhaps not. Duty wrestled with vanity, and vanity gained the fall.

"Can you see the road?" he asked, and there was no longer necessity to whisper.

"Oh yes," replied the girl on his right. "It's not so dark after all."

"The clothes you are wearing, are they warm enough, do you think, if you have to wait about for some time?"

"Yes. Besides, the night isn't cold."

"Good! Do you think you could walk for something more than a mile to the gate in the boundary fence?"

The left-hand girl cried emotionally:

"Walk! Oh, I could walk for miles and miles and days and days. Don't you see, we are free, free, free. Oh, thank you for getting us away from those horrible people." She altered her steps to walk in unison, and her slippered feet sang with happiness. The right-hand girl pressed his arm against herself, and the three of them swung along the road.

"I'm glad to hear you say that," he said, "because I shall not be able to go with you all the way. It's now nearly two o'clock. In another four hours it will be light, and I am hoping that before day breaks the police will arrive in force, for there will be plenty of them. If you follow this road for a mile you will come to a large gate in a tall wire fence. Now this side of the gate, about twenty feet, you will see across the road a narrow black ribbon. That's made of metal, and when you both stand on it the gate will open. When the gate is wide open you must run through the gateway, and then the gate will close again. Do both of you understand that?"

"Yes. We stand on the metal ribbon across the road and the gate opens long enough for us to go through."

"That's it. Now a little time after I leave you to go back to the homestead, I want you both to sing, and keep on singing until you reach the gate. Not loudly, but softly. Unfortunately you will not see the gate in the darkness until you are actually against it, but it is essential that as you approach the gate you will be singing, softly singing."

"All right! But why?"

"Because a friend of mine will, most likely, be waiting outside the gate, and if he doesn't know you are you he might throw a stone or something. Glen Shannon is, unfortunately, or perhaps fortunately, a trifle impulsive."

"I'm going to love that boy," announced the right-side girl.

"I've loved him a long time," announced the left-side girl. "You remember, Beryl, that I loved him first."

"I'll never forget it. You've done nothing else but din him into my ears for years and years." She braked Bony to a halt. "But why are you going back? If the police are coming, why go back there? They might shoot you. They would, I think."

"I won't give them the chance to shoot me," Bony boasted. "And besides, I want to hear that woman singing again."

"That was Miss Cora Benson, the lady who stands by and counts the lashes," asserted Mavis Sanky, bitterness making her attractive voice hard. "She was singing that German song, 'Lilli Marlene'. She *can* sing, I'll admit. Have you a pistol?"

"I have two."

"Then let me have one, and I'll go back with you and help somehow."

"You might shoot someone."

"I want to shoot that Heinrich."

Bony gently urged them into walking towards the gate and, he greatly hoped, Glen Shannon.

"Leave Heinrich to me," he said soothingly. "Don't think back. Don't permit your experiences here at Baden Park to weigh upon you. Ahead is the gateway to freedom and life and love. Go on from the gateway and leave the nightmare behind."

He felt Beryl Carson shudder. She was the slighter of the two and, as he knew from observation, mentally the tougher.

"Have you ever been flogged?" she asked, and he answered:

"No. But I have discovered that I am capable of flogging. Now, no more of this. The gate is a mile distant, and I must leave you. If Glen Shannon is not there, go on beyond the gate and up the road for some distance and then rest among the boulders. Wait there till daylight, for in the dark you cannot tell friend from enemy. I shall be wondering about you. Tell Glen Shannon he is not to enter Baden Park until the police arrive."

"We'll tell him, and don't you worry," one said, and the other asked:

"What's your name?"

"I am Detective-Inspector Napoleon Bonaparte, and all my friends call me Bony. I am hoping you will consent to be my friends."

"I wish it was light," said Beryl. "I'd like to look at you."

"I fear you would be disappointed. Now, we part here. Don't forget to sing softly. Au revoir!"

He was shocked when first one and then the other kissed him with a spontaneity indicative of gratitude and relief from oppression which words could not possibly express. He stood motionless on the road, listening. The homestead revealed no lights, no sound. He could no longer see the two girls, but he could hear them singing in unison, softly, beautifully. They were singing "Tipperary".

Twenty minutes later he was pressing his back against the observatory.

He could neither see nor feel any alteration in the picture. The recital, concert, or service, or whatever was going on, was still in progress. The door of the observatory was still ajar.

The organist was playing something languorous and soothing to the nerves, Bony's nerves, and he was feeling the benefit of respite following the second act of a tense melodrama. He had "sneaked" a cigarette made with the ends of those last cigarettes built with ends, and he would have experienced both pleasure and comfort in "sneaking" a square meal and a couple of drinks. He might have tried for one or the other and been lucky with both, did he know the position of the butler. Had he known this he would have made the attempt to return the key to its nail.

He estimated that he had been back at least ten minutes and, having remained inactive for a further ten minutes, he was prepared to gamble that Heinrich was within and not at the house for refreshments.

He took the chance and looked inside. He could see one of the women and several of the men seated in prie-dieu chairs, their backs towards him, and thus preventing identification. The chairs were a part of a line or row, the occupants facing towards a curtain of heavy swathes of alternating black and purple satin, concealing at least one-third of the interior of the building.

The organ was beyond the narrow range of his vision. The organist was playing softly a Johann Strauss waltz, and the people occupying the chairs were conversing.

The "curtain" inflamed Bony's curiosity. Itself, it was a thing of great beauty, tossing outward the light in shimmering waves of barred colour. Almost certainly beyond it was a stage, and no artifice ever invented to lure a famished mouse into a trap was more magnetic than was that curtain. Questions were like hammers. What was upon the stage? What brought these people here? Why was not the organ at one side or other of the stage? Why was it placed somewhat just inside the door?

The butler moved into Bony's range. He was gathering glasses. He had the hands of a boxer, the face of a burglar, the head of a typical Prussian.

Bony slipped away to cover as Heinrich came towards the door with his loaded tray.

CHAPTER XXVII

THE PLAY

As Heinrich crossed to the house, Bony wondered why it was that the man he had pushed under the bed had not been missed. It was more than an hour since he had dragged the body along the passage to the bedroom, and the only acceptable explanation was that Benson and his sister, as well as the butler, assumed the absent man to be doing something or other.

The girls should by now have reached the gate and passed outside, and Shannon should have been at the gate when they arrived. The escape had not been discovered and, therefore, the prison key had not been missed. Replacing the key, however, had been too long deferred, for these people must not be alarmed before the arrival of Inspector Mulligan.

Opportunity to replace the key was withdrawn when Heinrich, having stepped into the small hall, closed the side door. The house front was now an unrelieved void against the sky, and the situation for Bony was even more complicated, as he could not keep track of the butler's movements. No matter what his intentions, he had become an unknown quantity.

Several minutes passed, and Bony crossed to the house and tried the door, to find it locked. He had his hand still clasped about the door-handle when he caught movement outside the main entrance. Flat on the ground to obtain a sky-line, he saw the man. Heinrich had not put on a light in the main hall; he was walking swiftly across the circular space towards the outbuildings.

That Heinrich had missed the key seemed certain. Probably on finding the key not hanging from its nail he was in doubt that he had relocked the padlock fastening the bolt, or was thinking he might have dropped the key near the door. He would surely ascertain with his flashlight aimed through the barred window that the prisoners were not within.

Pistols, of course, were out of the question. They are old-fashioned when the success of an operation is dependent upon silence. Heavy-gauge fencing wire is more efficacious. As Heinrich stood before the prison door directing his light to the bolt, Bony was standing less than a dozen paces behind him.

Bony watched the butler look for the key about the ground before the door. Heinrich spent but a few seconds in this search before abruptly striding round the building to the window in the back wall. He was maintaining elevation at the window with one arm, whilst directing the beam of the flashlight inside with the other, when Bony slipped round the corner. He was still clinging to the high window, still searching the interior with his torch, when the wire hissed.

The wire neatly split the man's scalp at the back of his large head. It was not fatal, merely producing lights and a numbness down his neck and into his shoulders. He dropped to the ground, spun round, and dived the right hand into a side pocket. Then the wire hissed for the second time and fell downwise upon his face. The torch rose high in an arc, and Heinrich sucked in air to shout. Bony, who had leaped to one side to gain the proper angle for the *coup de grâce*, rendered it, and Heinrich, clawing at his throat, collapsed.

Bony jumped for the torch, switched it out, jumped back to the almost invisible body and listened. He heard nothing. Running round to the front of the prison, he stood there listening and regarding the bulk of the observatory with its two illumined windows high up in the wall. There was nothing to indicate an alarm, and he went back to Heinrich, finding the man lying upon his back, and then he committed the only mistake of the night. He did not assure himself whether the man was alive or dead.

Again at the front, the observatory windows led him to see a faint line of illumination indicating a skylight in the dome, and there were the iron rungs inset into the wall which would take him up to the line of illumination.

A minute later he was mounting the iron ladder which followed the curve of the dome beside a glazed skylight. Beneath the skylight were drawn linen blinds, and he went on up, hoping to find one not fitting and finding one not completely drawn. Lying upon the ladder and gazing down upon the incomplete tableau beneath the dome, he suffered disappointment.

He could not see the stage, for some dark material completely roofed it. He could see that the magnificent curtain had been drawn to either side and that three wide and low steps led upward from the auditorium. In a corner to the left of the door stood the great organ, with Simpson seated before its banked keyboard. He was playing, his head thrown back, the music score unread. The three observable walls were masked by heavy draperies in alternating ribbons of black and purple, and Bony could see the possibility of hiding behind one of the bulging folds if he risked stealing in through the door and was unnoticed by the organist.

The question tore through his mind: What of the actors? The girls had said that all the people at the homestead were seated about the dining table, with the exception of the two men expected back from Dunkeld and whom Shannon had killed. Of those at the table, he himself had accounted for one, and the butler was also accounted for. That left two women and eleven men. The two women and ten men were seated in a row approximately midway between the door and stage, and the eleventh man was playing the organ.

There could be no actors, no entertainers. The people below could not be watching a film play in such brilliant lighting. He could not see their faces clearly, but they were sitting passively and regarding something upon the stage.

The music ended with a series of thunderous chords and Simpson left the organ to occupy the end chair. After an appreciable period the man at the other end rose to his feet, and Bony knew him to be Carl Benson.

Benson walked to the stage and disappeared beyond Bony's view. He remained there for at least a minute—it might have been two—when he reappeared and resumed his chair. Bony counted twenty before Benson's neighbour, one of the women, rose and stepped up to the stage, so passing from Bony's view. She was there as long as Benson, returning to her chair with the stiff action of a sleep-walker. When her neighbour, a man, went to the stage, Bony realised the opportunity of entering the building and concealing himself behind the draperies.

On reaching the door, he could see four chair backs at Benson's end of the line. Those four chairs were occupied, and with great care he pushed the door farther inward until he could see the vacated chair and, between the chairs, the stage.

There were no actors other than a man in evening-dress standing with his back to the "audience".

Bony drew away. The man on the stage was turning round. He came down the steps, marched slowly to his chair, his face white, his eyes wide. A pause, and his neighbour rose and walked forward, and during that short walk Bony slipped in round the edge of the door and in behind the wall drapery, coming to rest with his back against the wall, where two sections of the drapery met and provided a fold.

He could part the draperies and look through, and now he had a clearer view of the stage and the chance to study it.

The back and sides were draped with cloth of gold. Dwarfing the man standing with bent head, and seemingly about to fly out from the back wall, was a huge, black, double-headed eagle. The man was standing on the edge of a marble dais, and upon the dais was set a block of stone as green as uranium and semi-translucent. Upon the green stone rested a black casket with raised lid.

Simpson was the last to make the pilgrimage, for that is what it appeared to be, and on his return he crossed to the organ and began to play a portion of Wagner's tetralogy, the *Ring of the Nibelung*. Concluding, "Deutschland über Alles" was like a fluid of sound pouring about the company, now standing, as the curtains slowly moved to contact at centre.

When the last notes swooned into silence Benson raised one hand, and the reason for the signal Bony never knew, for in that instant there broke into the silence the shrill ringing of a bell placed somewhere above the door. Benson's face registered leaping anger, Simpson spun round on his organ seat and joined the startled company. The bell continued ringing imperatively, not to be denied. Benson glared, took in the company as though counting heads and shouted:

"Where is Heinrich? Jim, find out what your people want."

The bell stopped as Simpson strode to the door which Bony had been careful to leave ajar. He pulled back the door and Heinrich almost collided with him as he staggered in, gazing wildly about like a man both blind and drunk, and, on seeing Benson, tottered forward.

"What is the matter with you, Heinrich?" Benson demanded harshly, a seemingly unnecessary question, as Heinrich's head appeared to have been mauled by a chaff-cutter.

The man swayed drunkenly upon his feet, tried but failed to articulate, closed his eyes as though about to faint, and then, with all credit, exerted tremendous effort to remain upright. No one offered assistance. No one brought him a chair. Not one of those astounded by the appearance of the man was more astounded than Napoleon Bonaparte. The man who had given the toast spoke:

"With your permission, Carl, I will attend to Heinrich. Odgers! Assist Heinrich to the house."

Benson said, as though the butler's state was of minor importance:

"Thank you, Dr. Harz. Jim, did I not say—— The telephone, quickly. Ladies and gentlemen, please return to the house. Conrad, be pleased to have your aeroplane in readiness for flight."

The sound of the butler's dragging feet on the gravel came in through the open doorway as the last of the company passed from Bony's range of vision. He heard a woman say:

"Why was not Bertram with us this evening?"

"He complained of a sick headache, Cora," replied her brother. "He said he would r-tire and take aspirin and join us when he felt better. His absence may now be significant. We must——"

The voice faded, was cut off by a slight thud. Air pressure informed Bony that the door had closed.

He listened and could hear nothing. Without disturbing the draperies, he was unable to see the door or the organ beyond it. He was waiting tensely, holding his breath the better to hear, was concluding that he was entirely alone, when the lights went out. He relaxed, leaning back against the wall, his mind winnowing facts from impressions and classifying probabilities and possibilities.

Benson had ordered Simpson to find out what his people wanted, and it was certain that the order was connected with the ringing bell, although it had not sounded like a telephone bell. It meant that someone at the hotel was calling up the homestead and that the instrument in the house actuated the summoning bell in the observatory.

Who could be ringing from the hotel? Unless Mrs. Simpson and her daughter had returned, who else could be there? Only the old man, and he could not leave his bed. It would not be

Mulligan, for even if Mulligan was thus early he would not make that mistake.

Glen Shannon! Improbable, because Shannon ought to have returned from Dunkeld, ought to have opened the double gates for Mulligan, ought to have reached the Baden Park boundary gate long before this. Perhaps the bell had not been a telephone summons, but an alarm set off by Shannon tampering with the boundary gate, trying to gain an entry in readiness for the arrival of the police cars.

Bertram! No, because Bertram was dead. Of that there was no doubt. He ought to have made equally sure that Heinrich was dead before leaving him at the back of the prison hut. He had then made a mistake which might be costly before the night was out, for doubtless they would get the butler to talk, or write if he could not speak, and tell what had befallen him.

Time! He wondered about the time, how close it was to daybreak. How long had he been here? It might be almost four o'clock, perhaps after four, and at any minute Mulligan would arrive to go through the place like a tornado and sweep everyone and everything into his net.

Before that happened Bony had yet more to do. He still had to uncover Benson's secret and the motives for abduction and murder and the hospitality extended to these obviously German people. That upon the stage might inform him.

Within and without the observatory the silence was unbroken as he slid along the wall, parting the draperies with his hands so that they fell into place. Coming to the door, he felt for a handle or pull, found neither, discovered how closely the door fitted into the frame, decided that, like the gate, it was electrically controlled.

It was just too bad, for he would be a prisoner when Mulligan and his boys arrived. But—he was close to the hub of the mystery. An utterly fantastic idea had been simmering in his mind for an hour, but were it proved reality, for him fame would be undying.

He located the box of matches in one of his pockets, felt within the box, and found half a dozen matches and one fairly long cigarette end, of which he had no memory. He blamed himself for not having brought the butler's flashlight, despite the fact that he could not have foreseen how the situation would develop.

Aided by the flame of a match, he crossed the auditorium and was near the stage curtain when the match expired. With his hands he found the curtain, the cool surface of satin caressing his fingers. He found the parting, then the steps with a foot, passed up the steps, and permitted the curtains to fall back into place. Another match he struck and held high when the tiny flame had taken steady hold upon the splinter of wood.

Somewhere an engine was pumping water. The sound was monotonous, and he wished it would stop. It did not permit him to hear with the keenness demanded by the situation, for he must know instantly if the door opened and anyone entered the building. When the noise of a motor-engine came to him he realised that the pumping was that of his heart.

Before him towered the giant two-headed eagle, and between it and himself was the casket set upon the block of green stone. The match went out as he placed one naked foot upon the dais.

Striking another match, he turned to leave the stage, hesitated, and was for ever grateful that he did not make the second mistake in this one night. In the ensuing darkness he felt with a foot for the dais, stepped upon it, and slid forward, first one foot and then the other, until he encountered the uranium-green stone.

Owing to the power of the fantastic idea which had been with him for more than an hour, he mussed the striking of the next two matches and was left with only one.

Careful—careful, now. Hold the box and the match away from you, or the rain will put it out. Rain! It slid ticklingly down his face and gathered at the point of his chin, from which it dripped. Somewhere out in the warm and lovely night powerful aero engines puttered and hesitated, persisted and broke into rhythm.

He was successful with the match. Glass gleamed beneath the light in his shaking hand. He stooped over the casket, brought his eyes down to the glass, and the match down, too. Jewels winked with eyes of ice-blue and ruby-red. Beneath the glass was a man in uniform. The waxen face was heavy-featured, black-moustached. The vision faded, vanished.

The darkness was impenetrable, and yet the mind of Napoleon Bonaparte was illumined with other visions. He gazed upon newspapers in every corner of the world and saw his name. He stood or sat with people before radios all over the world and with them heard his name. All the world knew of him, the man who solved the world's greatest mystery.

Even in that moment the training of the half-aborigine did not falter. The spent match, like the others, and the now empty box were put safely into a pocket, and like a Cæsar setting forth on his triumph, he stepped from the stage and walked, without colliding with a chair, to the door.

He must show Mulligan, and not Mulligan alone, but Mulligan in company with witnesses, what he had discovered, why the two girls had been abducted and enslaved, why Edward O'Brien had been murdered and his body incinerated, why that fence had been built and to guard what.

But the door was shut and he was unable to open it. He must get out. This very instant. He must contact Mulligan before anything could happen to cheat him of eternal fame.

As he stood at the door, clawing at it to get it open, the lights flashed on.

CHAPTER XXVIII

THE GLORY FADES

TRAMPING men approached the door. The door opened and Bony took cover behind the wall drapery. Benson entered, followed by six men, stalwart and formal in evening clothes. Individually, none would have gained special notice among a gathering of business executives, but collectively they were distinguished by racial characteristics and bearing.

"To you, gentlemen, is the honour," Benson told them. "To you I am to transfer the Trust which has been mine for a year, and you are to conduct the Trust from me to those appointed to receive it.

"Captain Conrad will land the plane on a property I own near Portland. There a van will be placed at your service, and the van will transport the Trust and yourselves to a wharf at which members of my launch crew will be waiting. When the Trust and yourselves, with my launch crew, are transferred to the submarine, the launch will be sunk without trace.

"I beg of you, in your report to the commander of the submarine, to convey my regret that I failed to take every precaution to prevent any set of circumstances interfering with The Plan set for this twenty-eighth day of March, and, in consequence, being compelled to expose the Trust to unnecessary risks. As you know, The Plan included transport to Portland by road, as being the safest, and the enforced alteration to air transport will forward the time of boarding the launch by three hours, and the launch will be three hours early at the rendezvous with the submarine.

"Mrs. Tegen is to go with you. Ernst, who is to drive the van, and Wilhelm and Mrs. Tegen are now with the plane. Miss Benson will remain with me. So, too, will Heinrich and Simpson. We shall not live to be arrested. That is all."

Benson strode to the organ and pressed a button, which set in motion the mechanism controlling the stage curtain. Bony watched them mount to the stage, where Benson gently closed the lid of the casket. The six men took up the casket and bore it from the building, Benson leaving after them. Their feet scuffled on the gravel without, became as the feet of one man marching, marching . . .

It could not be permitted. At all costs to himself it must not be permitted. Bony tore himself free from the wall draperies and dashed to the door, no longer taking count of the interior lighting revealing him to anyone without.

The aeroplane engines were throbbing with smooth power. A car was approaching at terrific speed. The porch light was on. The house roof was etched against the sky, now paling with the advancing dawn. To the right, Benson's flashlight revealed the way to the bunched men carrying the casket.

The noise of the car engine drowned out the sound of the aeroplane as it entered the space before the house, skidded with locked wheels, rocked, and almost turned over. From it appeared Simpson, who rushed to the observatory door, looked in, turned, and ran for the house porch, on which stood Cora Benson.

"The gate was forced, Cora!" he shouted. "It was open. We got out and examined it. Someone jammed stones under it to keep it open. We were looking round when Heinrich fell. I heard the bullet slap him. They're using silencers. They shot at me too. It couldn't have been the same people who broke into the hotel and set off the alarm. Aren't you going? Come on—we mustn't miss the plane."

"I am not going," the woman said slowly, adding: "Neither are you."

"But I must go. I can't stay here. I can't——"

Leaving the porch, he ran along the house front to take the path after Benson and the bearers. His dress-coat was split up the back, and one shoulder of it hung down and flapped as he ran.

Bony followed. He could have winged Simpson and arrested him for the murder of Edward O'Brien, but who and what was Simpson now compared with the contents of that casket being borne along the garden paths to the waiting aeroplane? Simpson was shouting to Benson, and Bony could hear his voice, panting, imploring, fearful.

"You must let me go too, Carl. There was someone there at the gate. Heinrich got it. They're using silencers. They've propped the gate open with stones ready for the police cars. I can't remain here, not now, Carl. I can't go back to the hotel."

"No, Jim, you can't go back to the hotel," Benson said coldly. "And you cannot go in the plane."

"But I must, Carl. The police will know everything. They'll know about those girls who've escaped, know how you and Cora forced them to work. They'll get to know about Ted O'Brien. I didn't tell you, but I thought I saw that someone had been in the place where I buried him. I tell you they'll get to know everything, even about Price and how he was shot at your orders."

The small procession halted at the garden gate whilst Benson opened it. Beyond it the new daylight was drowning the night on the floor of the valley. Bony stopped, waited for the bearers to get clear of the gate that he might detour round them to reach the plane and disable it with bullets fired into the revolving propellers. The procession passed through the gateway and Simpson resumed his frantic pleading.

"Let me go, Carl! Let me go, please, please. I've given everything to the Trust, done everything. We must all go, you and Cora and I. The police——"

"You cannot go, Jim. The plane will be fully loaded, and the Trust is not going to be endangered with overloading. You are the weak link in this organisation, which otherwise would have been perfect. We've both made mistakes. We both have to pay the price, I within a few minutes, you now. Was Heinrich shot dead?"

"Yes. I'm certain of that. Cora——"

"Cora will never fail. Nor will I. You would, and so——"

There was a spurt of flame and a sharp report. Simpson stumbled, lurched forward, tried to keep up, fell. Benson stooped over him and fired again with the weapon pressed against his friend's head. The bearers did not falter. They went on to the aeroplane standing about a hundred yards distant from the gateway.

The light was strong enough to observe a running man, strong enough for Benson to dispense with his torch. Out here beyond the garden were no trees to retain the darkness, and Bony had to pass the bearers to get at the plane. The range beyond the valley curled its crests to greet the dawning, but the beauty of it was not registered on the mind of a man seeking for cover in which he could pass the bearers. There was no cover other than the white-painted post-and-rail fence erected to keep stock back from the swirling creek.

Without sound Bony raced to the fence, intending to run along its far side to the machine waiting quite close to it. The fence appeared strong. Lady Luck struck cruelly. The rail gave beneath his weight as he vaulted it, splintering with noise.

"Go on," shouted Benson. "Wait for nothing. I'll keep this fellow pinned."

Bony had heard the snap of the bone in his left arm, but he felt no pain as he rolled over upon his chest to see Benson emerge at the rear of the bearers and begin to run towards him. Benson dropped, sprawled forward, opened fire, sent a bullet into the post behind which Bony had instinctively taken cover.

Again Benson fired and again the bullet thudded into the fence post, and the post was only five inches in diameter. Bony tried to shrink his body, and he wanted to yell when a giant's stick lashed his side. The pain passed and his body felt numb. Another pain tore upward the length of his broken arm, and with all his will power he thrust aside that pain to concentrate on aiming at Benson.

Benson was inching towards him. Beyond Benson a great area of tenuous mist about the electrically-controlled gate was flooded with the lights of Mulligan's cars. Benson fired again, and Bony heard the sound of the pistol and felt the wind made by the bullet as it passed through the inch-wide corridor between his face and the post.

The plane's engines burst into louder song, but he dared not look at it. Benson was less than forty feet away, calm, cold, fearless, aiming with dreadful precision, and Bony had to roll himself away from the post to rest on the good right arm that he might aim at Benson.

Benson's next bullet entered his left leg above the knee, and it felt as though the leg had been neatly torn away. He saw Benson's white face and steadied himself, held his breathing and fired. He wanted to shout his exultation when Benson sank into the grass and did not move. For four seconds Bony watched him and knew Benson would never move again.

The exultation passed as swiftly as it had seized him. The

bearers were passing the casket up a short ladder to those in the plane. A man was crouched before one of the landing wheels. The spinning propellers were like a flight of dragon-flies at the level of the eastern range crests. There was still time to reach the machine and fire into those revolving discs.

Despite the one broken arm and the one useless leg, he managed to drag himself up the post to the rail and then half lie over it. The ground was shuddering. It was all passing from him: valley, aeroplane, men, homestead. That wretched rail on the far side of the post had beaten him, robbed him of most of the glory. If only he could move nearer to the machine. He might . . . He tried to slide his body along the railing. The police would get the casket. Mulligan would have every police-man south of Baden Park on the look-out for the aeroplane. It would have to land somewhere—near Portland, Benson had said. The police would stop the van before it reached Portland, stop them from transferring the casket to the boat. The police at Portland would be waiting for the van, warned, instructed by telephone.

But, to use Benson's words, not to him would be the honour of presenting the casket and its contents to the world through Mulligan; of saying to Mulligan and his men: "This was the motive for the abduction of two young women, of the murder of Detective Price, of the murder of Yardman O'Brien. This . . ." and raising the lid of the casket to let them see who rested under the glass.

His left arm was a great weight, almost more than he could continue lifting with his shoulder. The leg wasn't so bad, but a man couldn't do much with only one leg, in addition to only one hand and arm. His clothes on the left side of him must be on fire and were scorching him. How far away was that plane? Eighty yards! Perhaps he could put a bullet into it from eighty yards. He must try that. The men with the casket had disappeared, had passed up the ladder. A man was removing the wheel chocks. Then he was running to the ladder. Now he was going up the ladder. He kicked the ladder away and it fell to the ground. The aeroplane was alive. The ground was shuddering and it rocked the fence railing. The noise was terrific. The range was blotted out by wings. Only the sky was still. And in the sky was the aeroplane, flying over the house, turning away from it to head towards the range whose mighty wave crests were on fire. Smaller and smaller and turning from silver to gold, the machine dwindled to the size of a bee, which appeared to hover for a long time between the gilded teeth of the distant range. A cavern of the clouds received it.

Then Shannon was standing beside him, and the American's strong fingers were taking the automatic from his hand.

"Fetch Mulligan," Bony said tonelessly.

"Mulligan's on the job," Shannon told him. "You're in a bad way, pal. Better come off the fence and lie down. Where did you get it?"

"Never mind me, Shannon. Bring Mulligan—quick."

"Don't worry, Bony, old pal. Mulligan's headed this way. There's cops all over the scenery. I'll lower you down. Smashed leg, eh! Clothes full of blood, too. Busted arm as well. Just take her easy. Wish't I'd come sooner. Me and the girls followed Simpson on the bike, but what a hope of catching up with his Buick. Left the girl friends getting a little of their own back on the Benson woman. Aimed a gun at us, and I knocked it out of her hand with a throat slitter. Then Mavis grabbed the gun. Left her itching to pull the trigger, and the other one urging the Benson woman to do something to give an excuse. Let's get your coat off and find out what's doing."

The sun had set and it was growing dark. He heard Mulligan's voice and he struggled against a yielding something which held him close. He must tell Mulligan—about the casket, where they were taking it. He heard Mulligan say:

"What's this? Inspector Bonaparte? Is he dead?"

He tried to tell Mulligan, but no one heeded. He could not see Mulligan or Shannon, and he wished Shannon would shut up and let him speak. He must tell Mulligan about the casket before—before . . .

Shannon's voice seemed far away:

"No, I guess he ain't dead yet. He's a real guy. Hit three times and still shooting at aeroplanes. What a guy! What a pal! There's twenty million cops in the world, and of the lot he's the only pal of the Shannons of Texas."

He dreamed much and often. Faces appeared in his dreams. Many he did not recognise, but among them were the faces of Superintendent Bolt, Inspector Mulligan, Glen Shannon, and one girl who had glorious auburn hair and another whose face was very beautiful.

When he awoke from his dreams the first thing of which he was conscious was of being in bed. Well, there was nothing so remarkable in that, because beds were invented to sleep in. Then into the white ceiling swam a face in which were two of the bluest eyes he had ever looked into, a face crowned with a nurse's veil.

She smiled down at him and he tried to smile at her. Then he went to sleep, and the next time he awoke there was another nursing sister who came to bend over him, and her eyes were large and grey.

"What is the date, Sister?" he asked.

"Don't bother your head about dates. Don't talk—not yet."

"What is the date, Sister?" he again asked.

"Well, it's the fourth of April," she conceded. "Now just lie quiet. Doctor will want to see you. Please don't fret."

She watched his eyes cloud and she thought her patient was about to weep. When she saw his lips moving and the effort to speak, she thought it wise to listen and soothe.

"Did they trace the plane, Sister?" he asked weakly, and she answered:

"Yes. It was found near Portland. It was deserted and none of those on board have been found, as far as I know. Now you really must not talk any more, and I must fetch Doctor."

"Your finest achievement, Bony," Superintendent Bolt told him the next day. "Finding those two girls and getting them away was damned good work. The newspapers are full of it. Like us, they're raring to know the whys and wherefores. You just take your time and tell your old pal about it. Must have been quite a ruddy war."

"You did not arrest the people who got away in the plane?" Bony asked.

"No. The machine was landed on a farm owned by Benson seven miles out from Portland. It wasn't located until the afternoon of that day it flew from Baden Park, because Mulligan had to go as far as Dunkeld to communicate. Telephone wires were cut in half a dozen places, and that caused vital delay. Having found the plane, enquiries resulted in learning that a van had unloaded a large box and several men into a small boat, which took all hands and their box to Benson's ocean-going launch, which at once put to sea. The next day a sea-search was made for the launch with boats and planes, but it was not sighted. They're still hunting."

"Just too bad, Super, that I couldn't stay on my feet long enough to report to Mulligan. What of the Benson woman? Did they take her?"

"Yes. But she won't talk, and we can only charge her with abduction—so far."

"What did they get from Shannon?"

"Nothing but Mavis, Mavis, Mavis. Says he won't crowd you."

"You are not holding him, are you?"

"No. Oh no. He's being married this morning. Mulligan's taking time off to be his best man. Now tell us the story—or I'll bust."

In fair sequence Bony related his experiences from the time he had entered Baden Park by the back door, the only item not included being what he had seen in the casket; that fantastic idea, that face he had seen with the aid of a spluttering match, that glimpse of the unbelievable.

"They were a bad lot, all right," Bolt continued. "Old Man Simpson was nearly frightened to death when Mulligan and his crowd went through the hotel. The fright made him properly balmy, poor old bloke. Mulligan says the place was wired, and they hadn't been inside more'n a minute when they found that their entry raised the alarm at Baden Park. There was nothing else, no evidence worth a hoot. Now, Bony, please tell your pal what was in the box."

"I don't know, Super."

"Oh yes, you do."

Bony closed his eyes as though he were tired, as, indeed, he was.

The sister intervened, saying that her patient was exhausted and that the Superintendent must go. Bony looked up into the troubled face of a man for whom he had great respect and not a little liking and he said:

"I can make a couple of guesses what was in the box, Super, and perhaps when we have both retired I may tell you what those guesses are. Had I been able to capture the box and its contents, the world, I think, might have been startled.

"I made a very great mistake when I guessed I had killed the butler, Heinrich, and I am not making another mistake by guessing. Had I made certain whether Heinrich was dead or alive, and, if alive, had taken measure to incapacitate him, he would not have turned up to give the alarm. Ah me, Super! I am a vain fool. If only I had not attempted to grab all the glory. If only I had waited for Mulligan."

"What was in the box?" pleaded Superintendent Bolt. "Tell us your guess. Go on—be a sport."

"Well, Super, I have the idea—the idea, mind you—that the contents of that box were of supreme importance to Benson and his associates."

Bolt sighed. He shook his head and said with exaggerated emphasis:

"You're telling me."

He watched the smile flit into Bony's eyes, and he heard Bony say with slow and equal emphasis:

"You have, I fear, been associating with Glen Shannon from Texas."